STORY PROGRAM ACTIVITIES
FOR OLDER CHILDREN

Carolyn S. Peterson
and
Christina Sterchele

MOONLIGHT PRESS

Orlando, Florida

Moonlight Press
3407 Crystal Lake Drive
Orlando, Florida, 32806

Copyright © 1987 by Carolyn S. Peterson and Christina Sterchele

ISBN 0-913545-11-2

372.64   Peterson, Carolyn S.

          Story program activities for older children.
          By Carolyn S. Peterson and Christina Sterchele.
          Orlando, FL: Moonlight Press, 1987.

          Includes index and bibliography.

          1. STORYTELLING. I. Sterchele, Christina,
          joint author. II. Title

              ISBN 0-913545-11-2

Printed in the United States of America

CONTENTS

PREFACE

This book is designed to aid you in planning and conducting story programs for older children, specifically those between the ages of eight and twelve.

In *Story Program Activities For Older Children* we have included a variety of materials from picture books to participation stories. Songs and stories suitable for use with the flannel board also include full size traceable patterns with complete detailed instructions for making each puppet. Choral readings, dramatic activities, and action songs comprise a chapter filled with participation suggestions. An extensive bibliography lists picture books, sound filmstrips, and 16mm films appropriate for older children.

Noticeably absent from this book is information relating to traditional oral storytelling. While storytelling is the backbone of story programs for older children, it is far too complex and difficult a skill to be covered in a survey. We recommend that you study the following titles to acquire information on this topic.

Baker, Augusta and Ellin Greene. *Storytelling: Art and Technique*. Bowker, 1977.

DeWit, Dorothy. *Children's Faces Looking Up: Program Building For the Storyteller*. American Library Association, 1979.

Sawyer, Ruth. *The Way of the Storyteller*. Viking, 1962.

Shedlock, Marie. *The Art of the Storyteller*. Dover, 1951.

We hope that you will enjoy using the resources in this book and that you have as much fun sharing them with children as we have had.

CSP and CS

INTRODUCTION

"Once upon a time long ago in a far-off kindgom..." These magic words have transported generation after generation into other times and other places. Today's crop of media-oriented eight-to-twelve-year-olds are not exceptions; they too succumb to the charms of a good story.

Planning and presenting story programs for children in the intermediate grades can be both challenging and satisfying. Success often lies as much in the selection of the material as in its presentation. Regardless of the kind of program you prepare, you must carefully match it to the levels of maturity and sophistication of your audience.

Story Program Activities For Older Children contains a varied array of literature-related materials designed for use with children ages eight to twelve. It includes songs, stories, plays, and verse with suggestions for implementation. Full-size traceable patterns for flannel board characters and puppets accompany the text of many selections. The collection of participation activities includes choral readings, action songs, creative dramatics, pantomime, and interpretation. An extensive annotated bibliography lists picture books, 16mm films, and sound filmstrips which are appropriate to use with groups of intermediate girls and boys.

Following are eight sample outlines for multi-media story programs for older children, each containing suggestions for a variety of story activities. Most of these programs will require about 30 to 40 minutes.

SAMPLE STORY PROGRAMS

1. MUSIC

The Sorcerer's Apprentice -- puppet play

I Am a Fine Musician -- participation song

Patrick -- 16mm film

Troll Music -- picture book by Anita Lobel

2. NOODLEHEADS AND FOOLS

The Three Wishes -- picture book by Paul Galdone

Lazy Jack -- story with flannel board

The Deaf Woman's Courtship -- song with puppets

The Foolish Frog -- 16mm film

3. FABLES

Once a Mouse -- picture book by Marcia Brown

Frog Went A-Courtin' -- song with flannel board

The Town Mouse and the Country Mouse -- interpretative activity

The Miller, the Boy, and the Donkey -- shadow

puppet play

Don't Count Your Chicks -- filmstrip

4. SCARY STORIES

The Teeny Tiny Woman -- story with flannel board

Liza Lou and the Yeller Belly Swamp -- picture book by Mercer Mayer

The Ghost of John -- song sung in rounds

The Legend of Sleepy Hollow -- 16mm film

5. DONKEYS AND MULES

Sylvester and the Magic Pebble -- picture book by William Steig

Lazy Jack -- story with flannel board

Sweetly Sings the Donkey -- song sung in rounds

The Miller, the Boy, and the Donkey -- shadow puppet play

The Erie Canal -- filmstrip

6. MAGIC

The Five Hundred Hats of Bartholomew Cubbins -- picture book by Dr. Seuss

King Midas and the Golden Touch -- story with flannel board

The Sorcerer's Apprentice -- puppet play

Strega Nona -- 16mm film

FLANNEL BOARD ACTIVITIES

The flannel board activities in this section are selected to appeal especially to intermediate children. Included are a variety of folk tales and songs which are special favorites of older girls and boys and which are particularly well-suited for use on the flannel board.

To prepare the materials, trace the patterns using a light pencil and tracing paper. With carbon paper transfer the pattern onto posterboard or heavy white paper. Color each piece with crayons, felt pens, or paint. For variety trace items of clothing or specific properties and cut them out of colored construction paper or fabric. Glue them to the original pieces with rubber cement or diluted white glue. Outlining everything in black adds depth to the appearance of the flannel board pieces.

When the set of materials is completed for a story or song, prepare them to adhere to the flannel board. If the pieces are simply to be placed on the board one at a time, e.g., *A-Hunting We Will Go*, glue strips of flannel or felt or attach pressure sensitive felt tape to the back of each. If the story or song is more complex, e.g., *Teeny Tiny Woman*, it will require more sophisticated preparation. Some pieces must stick to other pieces. For example, the teeny tiny woman must stick to her bed and the coverlet must stick to her. For these pieces place on the front of one and the back of the other small pieces of velcro or Hook 'n' Loop colored to match the piece. Since velcro tends to hold very tightly, you may prefer to use a loop of removeable transparent tape or easy-to-remove double-sided tape.

After you have prepared the materials for your story, practice it many times to make sure that the flannel board does not interfere with your storytelling. Skillful use of attractive flannel board materials can embellish a story, dramatizing it in much the same way as with simple puppets.

FLANNEL BOARD SONG

FROG WENT A-COURTIN'

Frog went a-courtin' and he did ride, a-ha, a-ha.

Frog went a-courtin' and he did ride,

Sword and pistol by his side, a-ha, a-ha.

He rode right up to Miss Mousie's hall, um-hum, um-hum.

He rode right up to Miss Mousie's hall

Gave a loud knock and gave a loud call, um-hum, um-hum.

He took Miss Mousie on his knee, a-ha, a-ha.

He took Miss Mousie on his knee

And said, "Miss Mouse, will you marry me?" a-ha, a-ha.

"Not without my Uncle Rat's consent," um-hum, um-hum.

"Not without my Uncle Rat's consent,

I wouldn't marry the president," um-hum, um-hum.

"Where will the wedding breakfast be?" a-ha, a-ha.

"Where will the wedding breakfast be?"

"Way down yonder in the hollow tree," a-ha, a-ha.

"What will the wedding breakfast be?" um-hum, um-hum.

 "What will the wedding breakfast be?"

"Three soup beans and a black-eyed pea," um-hum, um-hum.

Then Uncle Rat gave his consent, a-ha, a-ha.

Then Uncle Rat gave his consent

And that's the way the marriage went, a-ha, a-ha.

First to come in was a spotted snake, um-hum, um-hum.

First to come in was a spotted snake,

He ate up all the wedding cake, um-hum, um-hum.

Next to come in was a bumblebee, a-ha, a-ha.

Next to come in was a bumblebee

Bringing his banjo on his knee, a-ha, a-ha.

The last to come in was an old tomcat, um-hum, um-hum.

The last to come in was an old tomcat,

Who said, "I'll put a stop to that!" um-hum, um-hum.

Frog's bridle and saddle are laid on the shelf, a-ha, a-ha.

Frog's bridle and saddle are laid on the shelf,

If you want any more, go sing it yourself, a-ha, a-ha.

--Traditional, adapted for the flannel board

Trace the patterns and transfer them onto posterboard or heavy white paper. Color as desired and outline in black. Arrange the pieces on the flannel board to correspond with the text of the song.

Frog

6

Miss Mousie

Uncle Rat

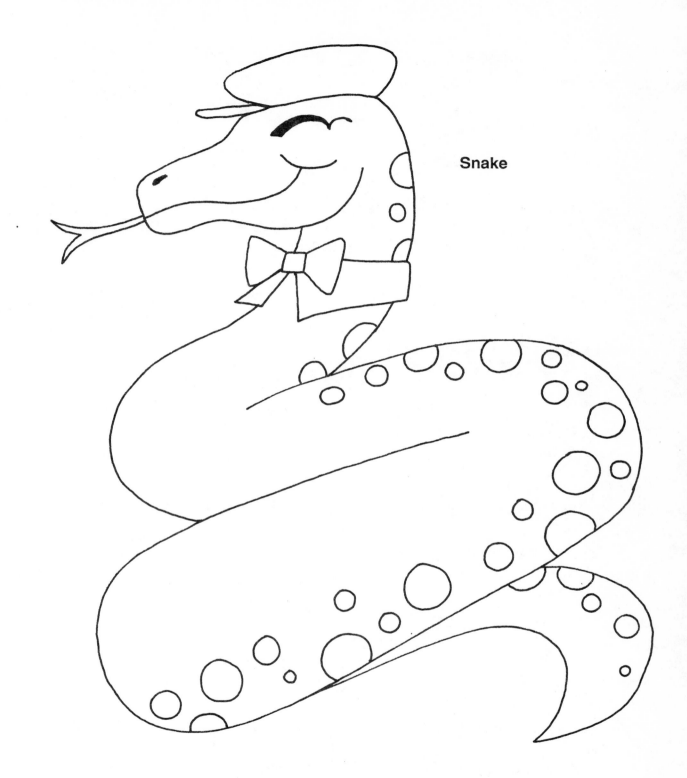

Snake

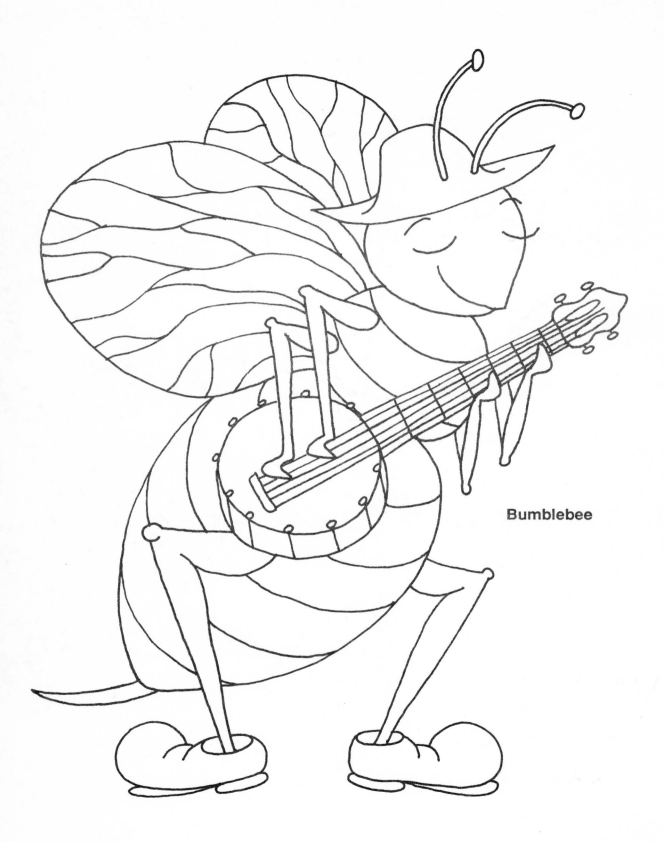

Bumblebee

Tom Cat

A-HUNTING WE WILL GO

Oh, a-hunting we will go, oh, a-hunting we will go.

We'll catch a little fox and put him in a box

And then we'll let him go.

Oh, a-hunting we will go, oh, a-hunting we will go.

We'll catch a little bear and put him in a chair

And then we'll let him go.

Oh, a-hunting we will go, oh, a-hunting we will go.

We'll catch a little mouse and put him in a house

And then we'll let him go.

Oh, a-hunting we will go, oh, a-hunting we will go.

We'll catch a little whale and put him in a pail

And then we'll let him go.

Oh, a-hunting we will go, oh, a-hunting we will go.

We'll catch a little duck and put him in a truck

And then we'll let him go.

*--Traditional, adapted for the
flannel board*

Trace each pattern and transfer onto posterboard or heavy white
paper. Color in bold, contrasting colors and outline in black. Place
each on the flannel board during the appropriate verse.

Fox in Box

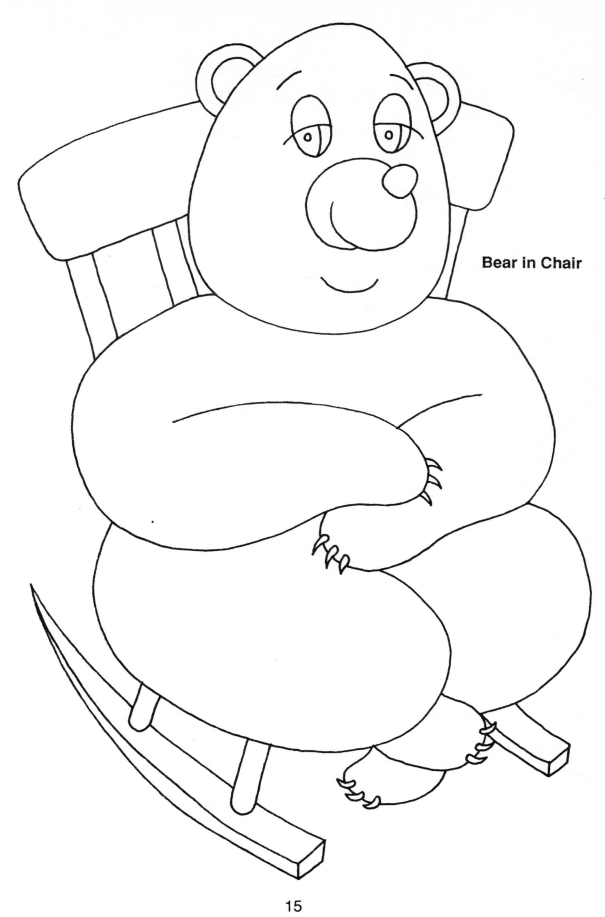

Bear in Chair

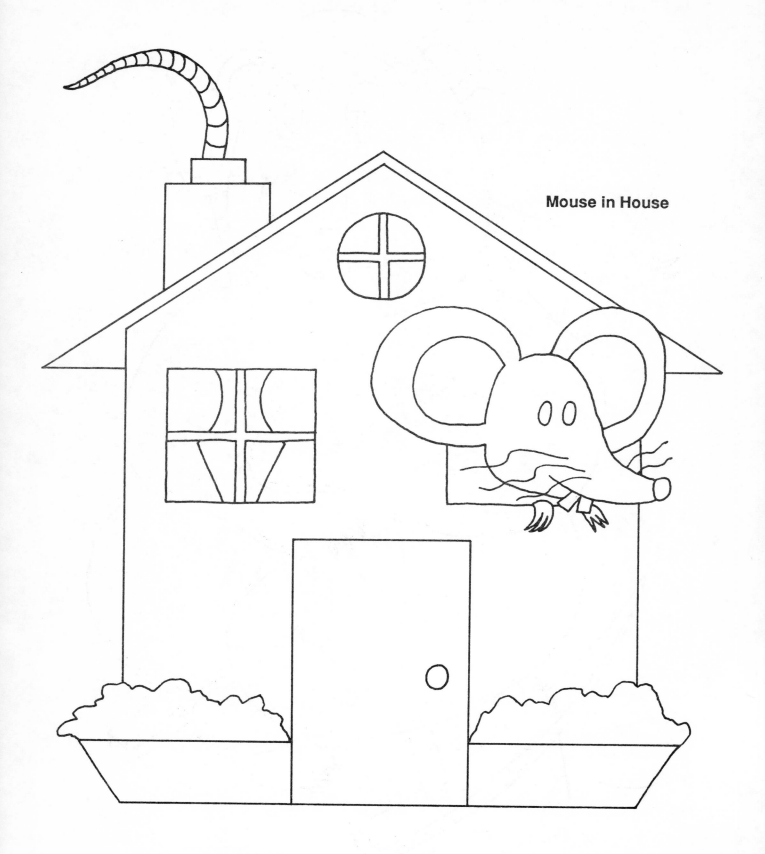

Mouse in House

Whale in Pail

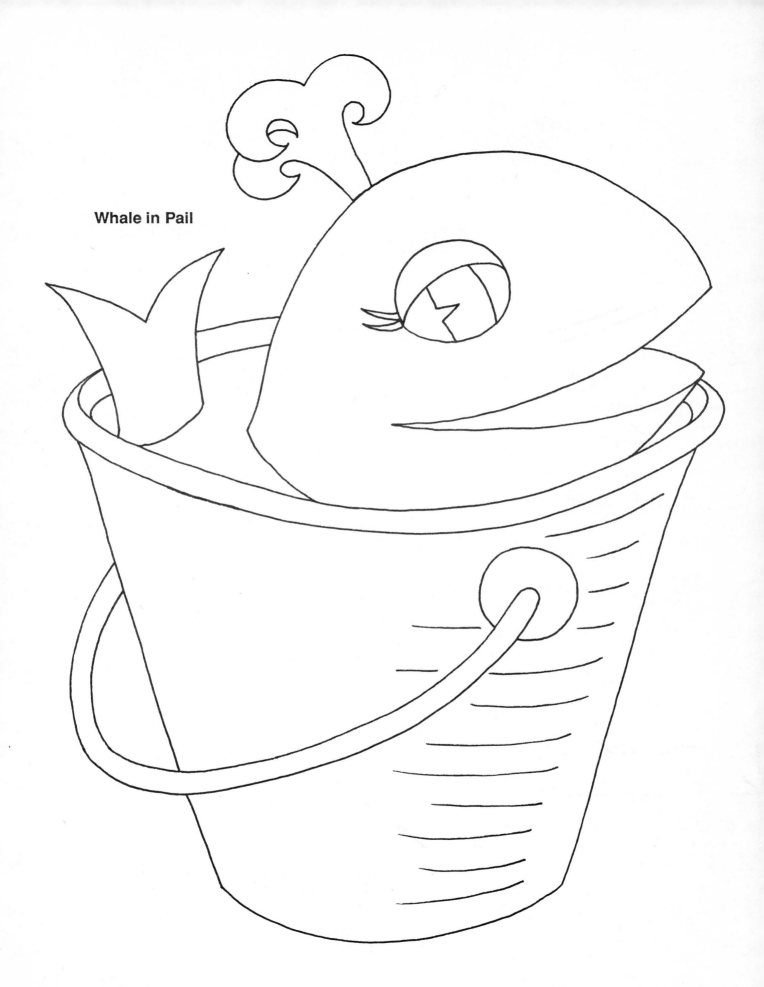

Duck in Truck

I AM A FINE MUSICIAN

1. like a trumpet

2. like a tuba

3. like a trombone

4. like a piccolo

I am a fine musician, I practice every day.

And people come for miles around just to hear me play

My trumpet, my trumpet, they love to hear my trumpet.

Ta-ra-ta-ta-ta, ta-ra-ta-ta-ta, ta-ra-ta-ta-ta-ta.

19

I am a fine musician, I practice every day.

And people come for miles around just to hear me play

My tuba, my tuba, they love to hear my tuba.

Oom-pah, oom-pah, oom-pah, oom-pah, oom-pah, oom-pah.

I am a fine musician, I practice every day.

And people come for miles around just to hear me play

My trombone, my trombone, they love to hear my trombone.

Dah, dah, dah, dah, dah, dah, dah, dah, dah, dah, dah, dah.

I am a fine musician, I practice every day.

And people come for miles around just to hear me play

My piccolo, my piccolo, they love to hear my piccolo.

Dee, dee, dee, dee-dle, dee, dee, dee, dee-dle, dee-dle dee, dee,
  dee-dee, dee-dle, dee.

*--Traditional, adapted for the
flannel board*

Sing the song with the children, making sure that they all know the words. Ask them to pretend to play each of the instruments. For a grand finale divide the group into four parts and assign each part a different instrument. Ask all four parts to sing their instruments simultaneously. Pictures of the instruments can be placed on the flannel board to serve as cues. Patterns for the four instruments appear on the following pages.

Trumpet

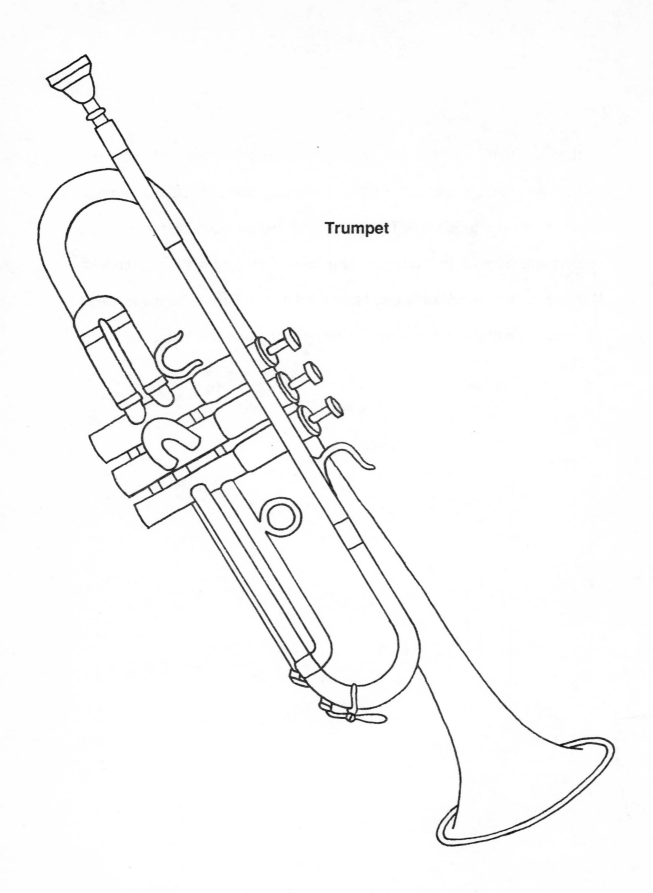

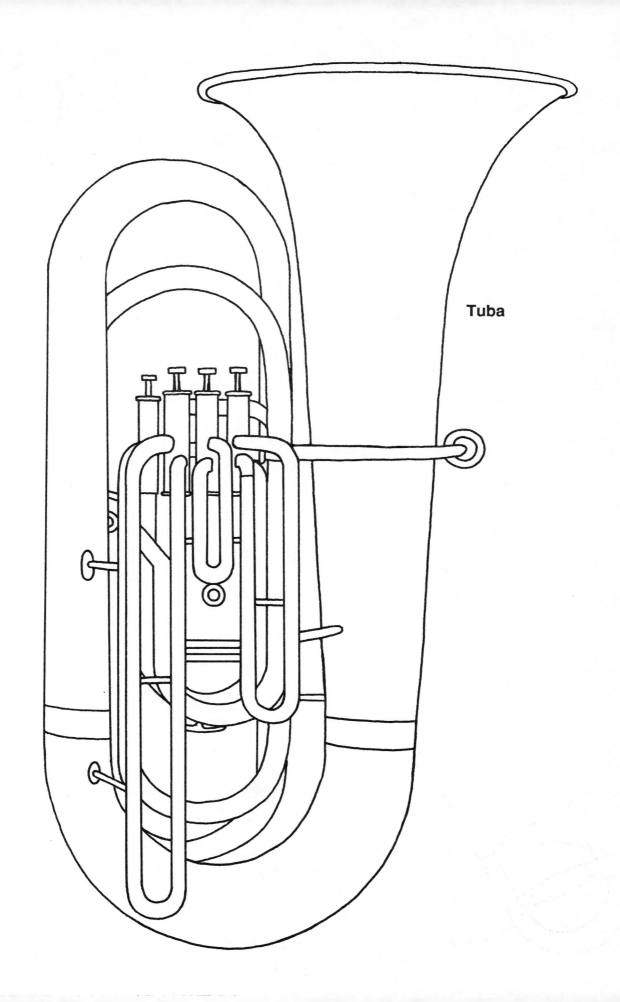

Tuba

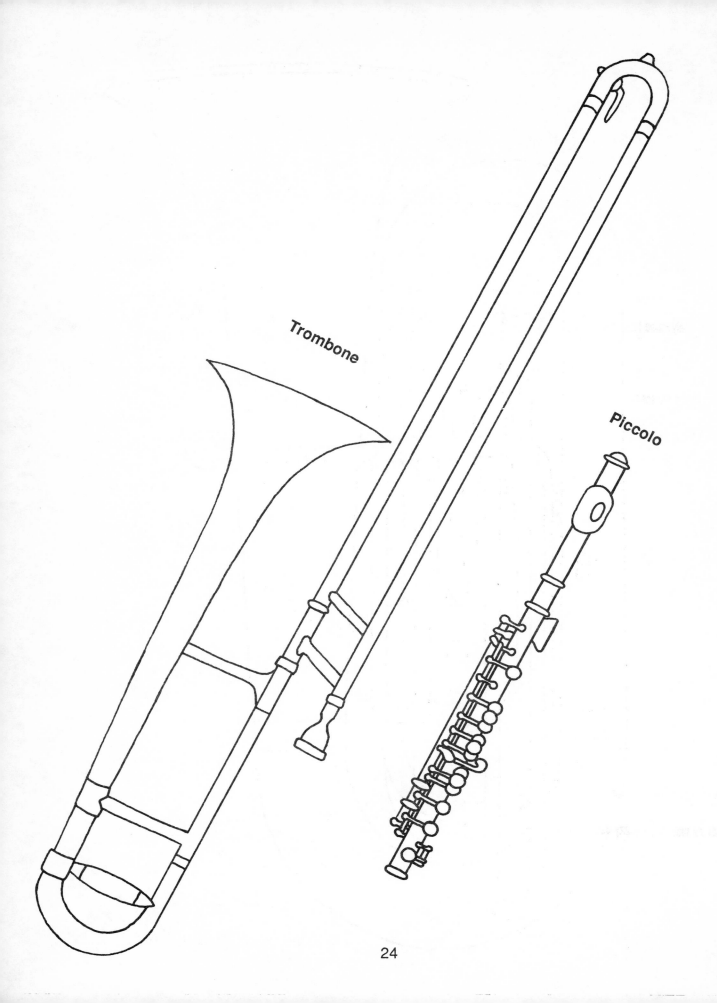

Trombone

Piccolo

24

LAZY JACK

Once upon a time there lived a poor widow who supported herself and her son by spinning. While she sat in the corner spinning from morn til night, her son, who was quite appropriately called Lazy Jack, lay dozing in front of the fireplace.

One day the poor woman could no longer endure her son's idleness. "Jack," she said, "a strapping lad such as yourself should be working to earn his own daily bread. You must go out tomorrow to seek work."

So Lazy Jack went out the following morning and found work assisting a farmer. At the end of the day the farmer paid Jack a coin, and Jack started home to give the money to his mother. Now Jack had never before had money, and, sure enough, he lost the coin as he crossed the brook.

"You fool!" exclaimed his mother. "Next time put what you earn in your pocket."

"I will, Mother; next time I will use my pocket."

The following day Jack hired himself out to a dairyman who paid him with a jug of milk. Remembering what his mother said, Lazy Jack carefully placed the jug in his pocket. By the time he reached his cottage, all the milk had sloshed out.

"Stupid!" cried his mother. "You should have carried the jug on your head."

"Next time, Mother, I will use my head," replied Lazy Jack.

Early the next morning Jack returned to work for the dairyman and that evening received as pay a fine cheese. Carefully, he placed it on his head just as he promised his mother he would. But the walk home was long and the evening was hot. By the time Jack arrived, the cheese had melted and run down over his face, his hair, and his clothing.

"You dunce!" yelled his mother. "You should have wrapped it in leaves and carried it in your hands."

"Next time, Mother," Lazy Jack lamented, "I'll wrap it in leaves and carry it in my hands."

The next day, Jack found work with the baker who paid him with a large tomcat. Lazy Jack dutifully tried to wrap it in wet leaves, but the cat spat and scratched until it wriggled from Jack's grasp and indignantly ran away.

"Dimwit," screamed his mother when he arrived home empty-handed. "Even a lazy dolt like you should have known better. Next time tie a string around its neck and lead it home."

"I promise, Mother," said Jack sadly, "that next time I will use a string and lead it home."

The butcher hired Jack the following morning. At the end of the day he gave the boy a large roast in payment for a day of heavy work. Mindful of his mother's advice, Lazy Jack carefully tied a string around the meat and strode off for home dragging the roast behind him.

"You simpleton!" shrieked Jack's exasperated mother. "Any fool would know to carry it on his shoulders."

"Yes, Mother," Jack sighed, "next time I will carry it on my shoulders."

His mother wrung her hands, "Oh, what are we to do? Five days you have gone out to work and we have nothing to show for it. Surely, next week you will be more careful with your earnings."

On Monday Lazy Jack set out at daybreak and hired himself out to a farmer. The farmer kept him busy all week long and on Friday rewarded him with a donkey.

To be sure, Jack was pleased with his wages and was eager to show his donkey to his mother. After considerable struggle, he managed to place the donkey on his shoulders and off he staggered for home.

Jack's journey led him through a village where there lived a wealthy nobleman and his lovely daughter who could neither speak nor hear. Doctors had declared that she could not be cured until she laughed. In desperation the nobleman had proclaimed that any man who could make his daughter laugh could have her for his wife and half the family's riches as well. Many a young man had tried and all had failed to make her laugh.

Meanwhile, Lazy Jack with the donkey dangling from his shoulders trudged through the village and past the nobleman's house. Hearing the sound of laughter, he looked up to see a beautiful girl leaning out the window, pointing at him, and laughing uproariously.

"Father," Jack heard the girl call between peals of giggles, "come and see the sight that is to be seen."

Hurrying to join his daughter, the nobleman could hardly believe that he was hearing her laugh and speak. Quickly, he sent servants out to bring Jack into his home.

"I never thought that my daughter would speak or hear. You, my friend, have cured her." The man clasped Jack's hand. "Would you like to have her for your wife?"

"If she is willing," replied Jack agreeably.

So Lazy Jack and the nobleman's daughter were married, and Jack inherited half the nobleman's wealth. Jack sent for his mother who lived with them in comfort and luxury. You can be sure that she never again referred to her son as Lazy Jack.

--Adapted for the flannel board

Trace the patterns on the following pages. Transfer onto stiff posterboard; color as desired and outline with black felt pen. Cut out. Glue flannel, felt, or other adhesive material to the back of each piece (commercial pressure-sensitive felt tape or removeable transparent tape will save time).

As you tell the story, place the appropriate pieces on the flannel board. Remember to remove each piece when it is no longer relevant to the story.

Jack (Top)

Jack's Hat

30

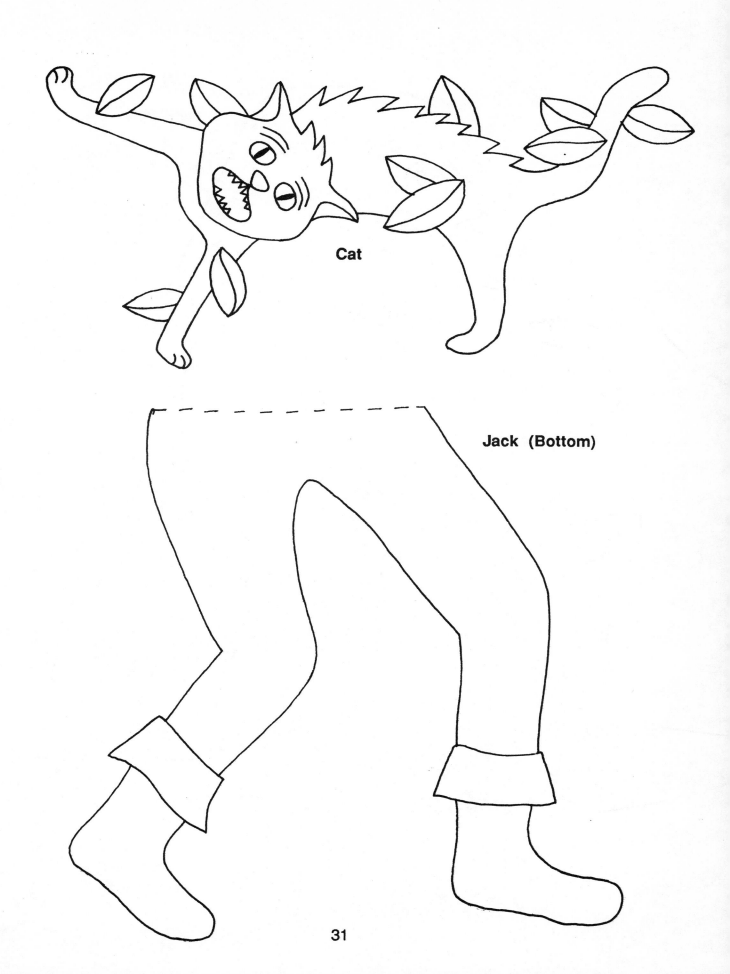

Cat

Jack (Bottom)

31

**Jack's Mother
(Top)**

32

Nobleman (Top)

33

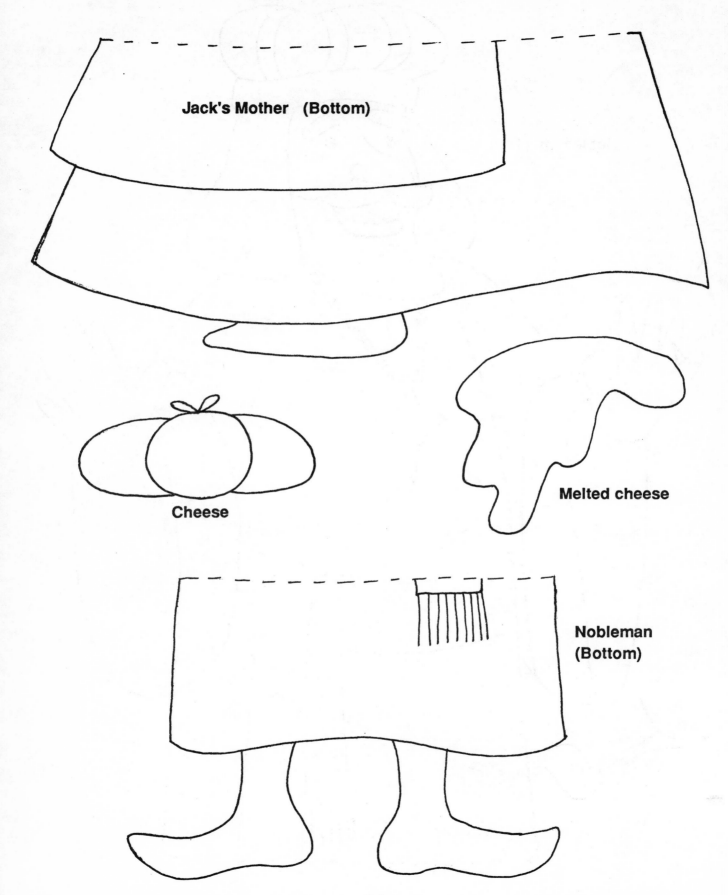

Jack's Mother   (Bottom)

Cheese

Melted cheese

Nobleman
(Bottom)

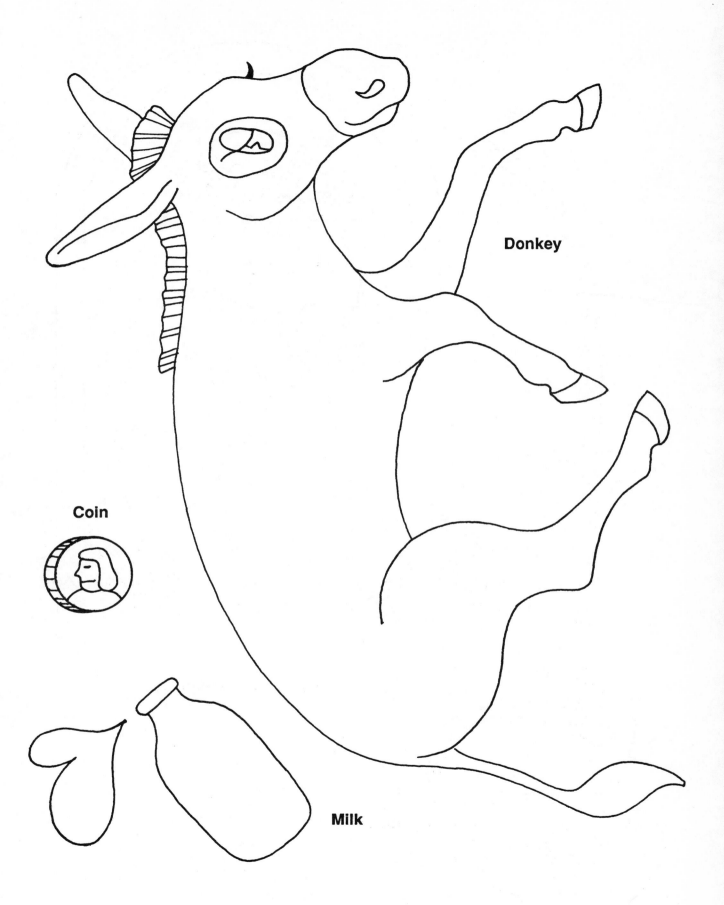

Donkey

Coin

Milk

Nobleman's Daughter

Roast

TEENY TINY WOMAN

Once upon a time a teeny tiny woman lived in a teeny tiny house in a teeny tiny village. One day the teeny tiny woman put on her teeny tiny hat, picked up her teeny tiny basket, and left her teeny tiny house to go for a teeny tiny walk.

The teeny tiny woman had gone but a teeny tiny way when she came to a teeny tiny gate. She opened the teeny tiny gate and walked into a teeny tiny churchyard. Inside the teeny tiny churchyard the teeny tiny woman saw a teeny tiny bone on a teeny tiny grave.

She said to her teeny tiny self, "This teeny tiny bone will make me some teeny tiny soup for my teeny tiny supper." So the teeny tiny woman put the teeny tiny bone in her teeny tiny basket, left the teeny tiny churchyard through the teeny tiny gate and walked home to her teeny tiny house.

When the teeny tiny woman reached her teeny tiny house, she was a teeny tiny tired, so she put the teeny tiny bone in her teeny tiny cupboard, and climbed into her teeny tiny bed.

The teeny tiny woman had been asleep but a teeny tiny time when she was awakened by a teeny tiny voice from inside the teeny tiny cupboard. The teeny tiny voice said, "Give me back my bone!"

Now the teeny tiny woman was a teeny tiny bit frightened, so she tucked her teeny tiny head under her teeny tiny covers and went back to sleep. When the teeny tiny woman had slept for a teeny tiny time, the teeny tiny voice again called from the teeny tiny cupboard, this time a teeny tiny bit louder, "Give me back my bone!"

This made the teeny tiny woman a teeny tiny bit more frightened, so she tucked her teeny tiny head a teeny tiny bit farther under her teeny tiny covers and once again went back to sleep.

The teeny tiny woman had slept but a teeny tiny time when once again she was awakened by the teeny tiny voice in the teeny tiny cupboard. It shouted a teeny tiny bit louder still, "Give me back my bone!"

This frightened the teeny tiny woman a teeny tiny bit more, but she pulled her teeny tiny head out from under her teeny tiny covers and said in a teeny tiny voice, "TAKE IT!"

--A traditional English tale
adapted for the flannel board

Trace the patterns and transfer them onto posterboard or heavy white paper. Color as desired and outline in black. Slit along heavy lines of cabinet's top two doors, leaving them connected on "hinged" sides so they can be opened to place the bone inside. You may wish to glue on beads for door and drawer handles to facilitate easy opening and closing. Arrange the pieces on the flannel board to resemble the teeny tiny woman's room. Place the tombstone to the far side of the board so that the woman can "walk" to it. Attach a strip of removeable double-sided transparent tape on the back of the bone so that it can be placed on the tombstone, in the basket, and inside the cupboard. Removeable tape or velcro should also be applied to the woman so that she can lie in bed and to the coverlet so that it will stay on the bed and can cover the woman.

Teeny Tiny Woman

Basket

Bone

REST IN PEACE

Grave

Hat

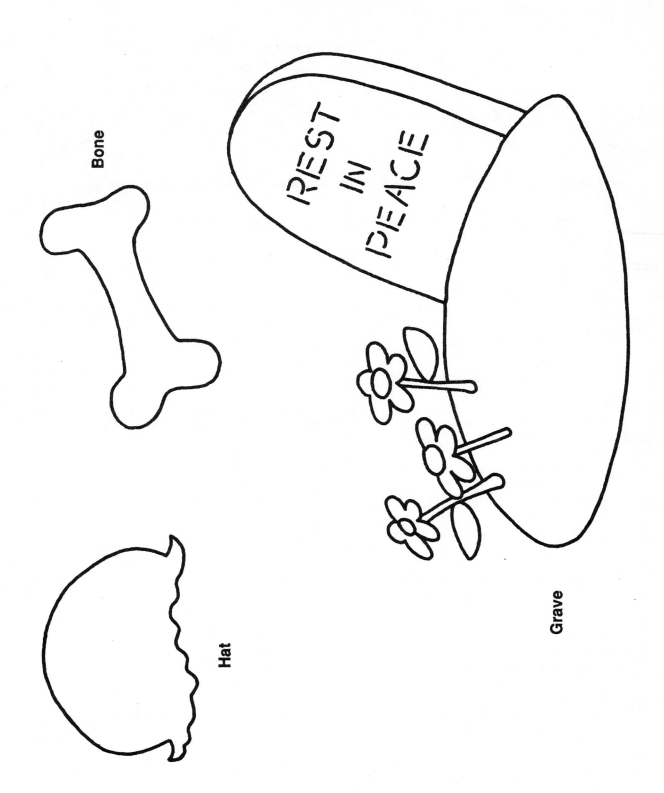

41

Cupboard

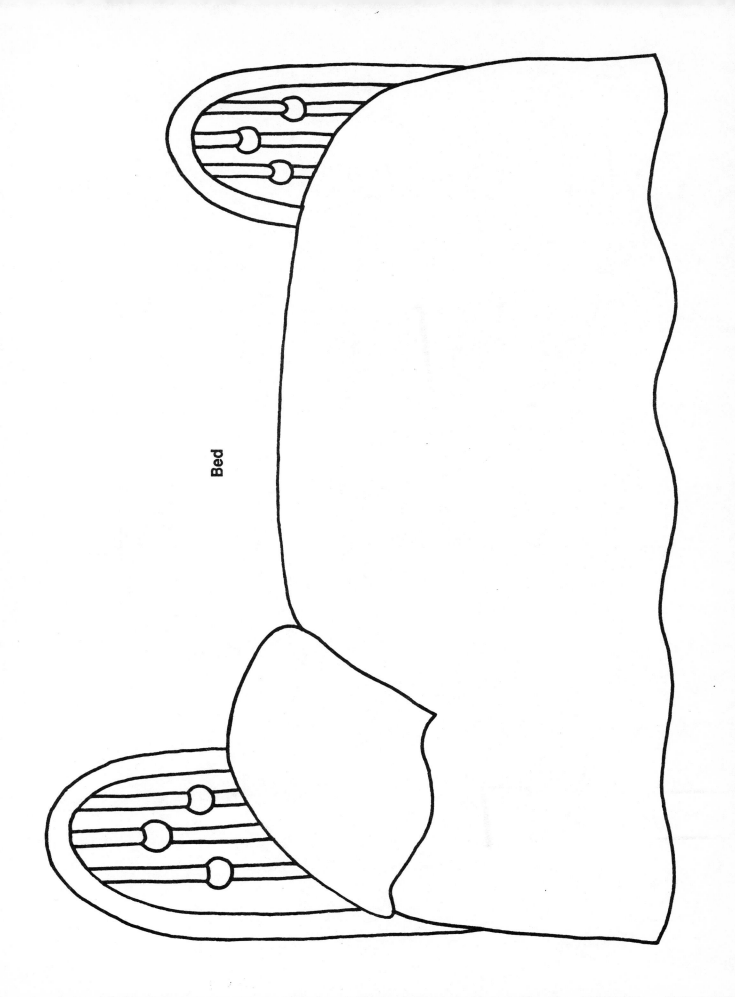

Bed

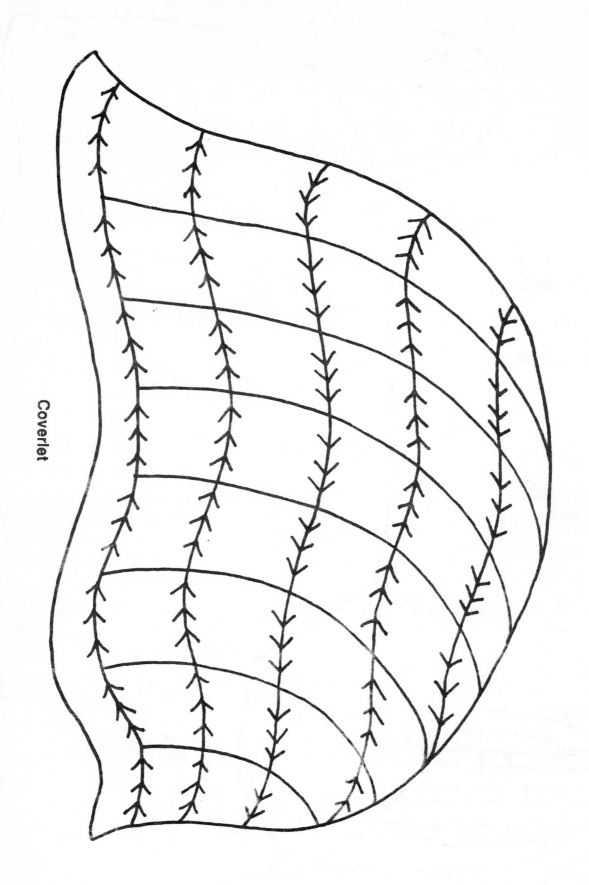

Coverlet

44

THE OLD WOMAN AND HER PIG

One day an old woman found a sixpence. "What shall I spend it on?" she wondered. "I think that I shall go to market and buy myself a pig."

On the way home from the market she came to a stile, but the pig would not go over it.

She went a little way until she came to a dog and she said, "Dog, dog! Bite pig. Pig won't go over the stile and I shan't get home tonight." But the dog wouldn't.

She found a stick and said, "Stick, stick! Beat dog. Dog won't bite pig. Pig won't go over the stile and I shan't get home tonight." But the stick wouldn't.

She went a little further until she came to a fire. She said, "Fire, fire! Burn stick. Stick won't beat dog. Dog won't bite pig. Pig won't go over the stile and I shan't get home tonight." But fire wouldn't.

A little further on she found some water. She said, "Water, water! Quench fire. Fire won't burn stick. Stick won't beat dog. Dog won't bite pig. Pig won't go over the stile and I shan't get home tonight. But water wouldn't.

She walked on until she came to an ox. She said, "Ox, ox! Drink water. Water won't quench fire. Fire won't burn stick. Stick won't beat dog. Dog won't bite pig. Pig won't go over the stile and I shan't get home tonight. But ox wouldn't.

Further on she met the butcher and she said, "Butcher, butcher! Kill ox. Ox won't drink water. Water won't quench fire. Fire won't burn stick. Stick won't beat dog. Dog won't bite pig. Pig won't go over the stile and I shan't get home tonight. But butcher wouldn't.

She went on until she found a rope and she said, "Rope, rope! Hang butcher. Butcher won't kill ox. Ox won't drink water. Water won't quench fire. Fire won't burn stick. Stick won't beat dog. Dog won't bite pig. Pig won't go over the stile and I shan't get home tonight. But rope wouldn't.

She went a little further and met a rat. She said, "Rat, rat! Gnaw rope. Rope won't hang butcher. Butcher won't kill ox. Ox won't drink water. Water won't quench fire. Fire won't burn stick. Stick won't beat dog. Dog won't bite pig. Pig won't go over the stile and I shan't get home tonight. But rat wouldn't.

Along came a cat and the old woman said, "Cat, cat! Kill rat. Rat won't gnaw rope. Rope won't hang butcher. Butcher won't kill ox. Ox won't drink water. Water won't quench fire. Fire won't burn stick. Stick won't beat dog. Dog won't bite pig. Pig won't go over the stile and I shan't get home tonight. But cat wouldn't. Instead she said, "If you will go to the cow and bring me a saucer of milk, I will kill the rat."

So the old woman went to ask the cow for some milk. The cow said, "If you will bring some hay, I will give you the milk."

The old woman went off to the haystack and brought back an armful of hay for the cow. After the cow had eaten the hay, she gave the old woman the milk. The old woman went at once to take the saucer of milk to the cat.

As soon as the cat drank the milk, she began to kill the rat; the rat began to gnaw the rope; the rope began to hang the butcher; and the butcher began to kill the ox. The ox began to drink the water; the water began to quench the fire; the fire began to burn the stick; the stick began to beat the dog; the dog began to bite the pig. The frightened pig jumped over the stile, and the old woman got home that night.

--Adapted for the flannel board

Trace patterns and transfer onto posterboard or heavy white paper. Color as desired and outline in black. Since this is a cumulative story, you may want to place the characters on the board at the appropriate time in the story and let them cumulate in a line as the story progresses. During the second half of the story, remove each piece after it has served the old woman. Your board will then be empty when your story is finished.

Old Woman

Dog

Stile

49

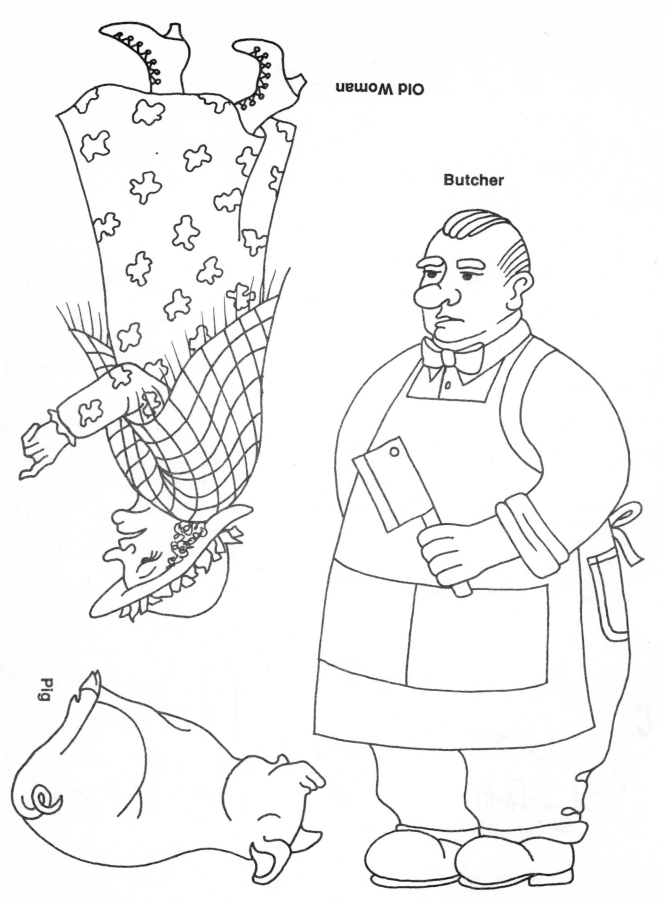

Old Woman

Butcher

Pig

50

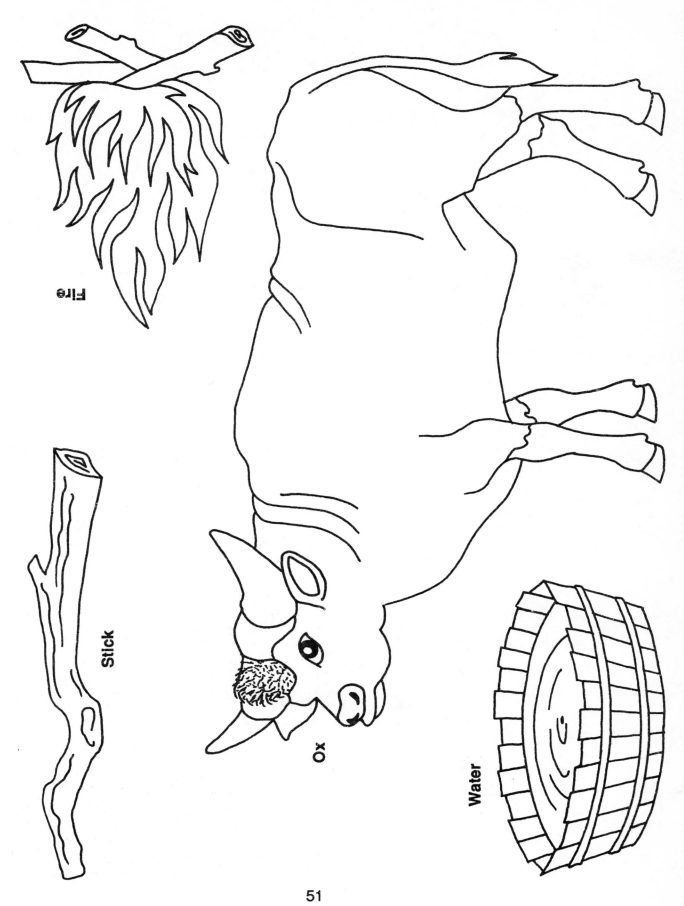

Fire

Stick

Ox

Water

51

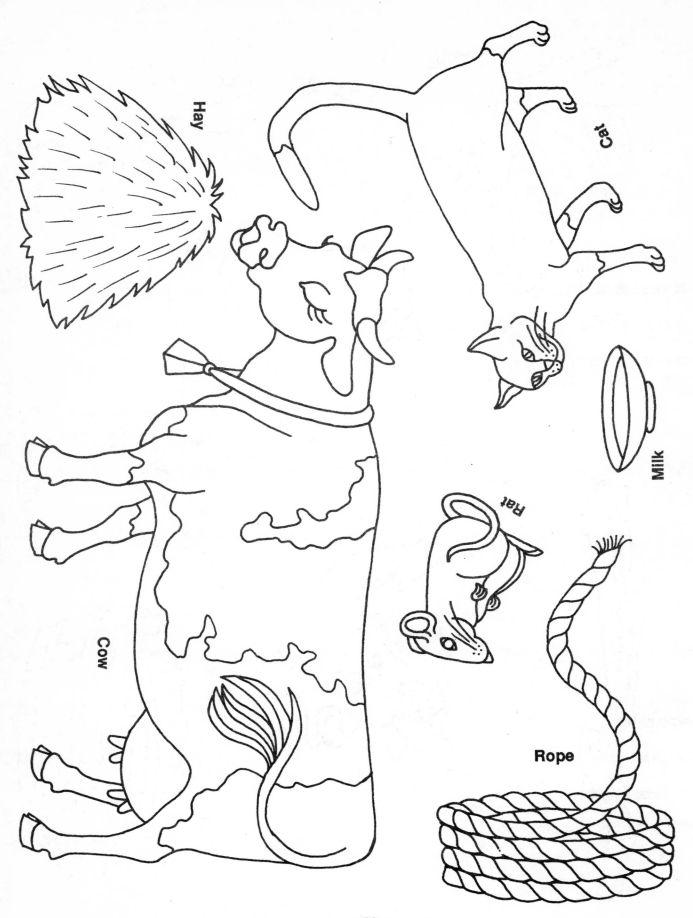

Hay

Cat

Milk

Rat

Cow

Rope

52

KING MIDAS AND THE GOLDEN TOUCH

Once long ago in a far away country there lived a king, Midas by name, who loved two things: his small daughter and gold.

His daughter, whom he called Marigold, was a lovely child with curling brown hair, dimples in both cheeks, and a sunny disposition. The king adored his little girl and spent hours with her in the castle and in the garden.

Each day, however, the king managed to spend time amid his treasure in a dreary, damp room beneath the castle. There he would sit holding first one bag of gold, then another. He would admire his reflection in the gleaming side of a huge gold cup; he would smile appreciatively as he sifted gold dust through his fingers.

Sometimes when he was in the garden with Marigold, she would run to him with buttercups or roses. After she had exclaimed over their delicacy and beauty, he might answer her in this fashion, "Ah, Marigold, would they were made of gold. Then they would be truly beautiful."

As weeks and months passed, King Midas spent more and more of his time with his treasure. One day as he sat surrounded by his piles of gold, he was startled by a glimmer of light and looking up saw a stranger in the room. Since Midas had carefully bolted the door, he knew that it was indeed no ordinary man.

"Ah, Midas," said the stranger, "you are truly a wealthy man, for surely no monarch exists who can boast of equal riches."

"Only middling wealthy," replied Midas sourly. "In perhaps 5000 years one might become truly rich."

"Only middling wealthy, Midas?" asked the stranger. "What would it take to make you feel as though you were truly a wealthy man?"

Midas propped his chin in his hand and slipped into deep thought. At length he replied, "If only I had the Golden Touch. Imagine how splendid if everything I touched turned to gold!"

The stranger looked at him wonderingly. "Are you sure, King Midas, that the Golden Touch would make you happy?"

King Midas rubbed his hands gleefully. "Oh, indeed, indeed," he replied.

"Very well, Midas. At sunrise tomorrow you will have the Golden Touch." And with that the stranger disappeared.

King Midas could hardly sleep that night. Over and over he wakened in anticipation of sunrise and the Golden Touch. At last his room was filled with a dim gray light and Midas sat up in bed. Breathlessly, he touched the goblet on the table beside his bed. Nothing happened. In disappointment he fell back upon his pillow. Had he only dreamed of the mysterious stranger? Surely the Golden Touch was too good to be true. At that moment a burst of light streaked the sky and Midas realized that only now had sunrise come. To his utter delight he saw that the coverlet clutched in his hand had turned to purest gold.

"The Golden Touch! I have the Golden Touch!" he cried. He leaped from bed and quickly touched the goblet, the table, a chair and each gleamed golden in the early morning light. He nodded approvingly as his clothes changed to gold cloth (although he admitted somberly to himself that they were rather heavy).

King Midas rushed to the garden and touched each of the roses blooming there and noted with satisfaction that each now was formed of exquisite gold.

In the midst of his excitement Midas remembered that it was breakfast time and that he was hungry. Returning to the castle, he sat down at the table to await Marigold. Momentarily, she burst into the room sobbing and carrying one of the golden roses.

"What is it, my child?" asked the king. "Why tears on such a glorious morning?"

"Look, Father," she sobbed, thrusting the rose at him. "All of the beautiful roses are spoiled! They have lost their sweet fragrance and their petals are stiff and hurt my nose."

Midas was ashamed to admit that he was responsible for the roses. Instead, he gently invited his little daughter to come and enjoy her breakfast.

As for the king, he enthusiastically filled his mouth with a large bit of hotcake. To his shock he found his mouth filled with a lump of gold. He tried a bit of egg only to have it also become solid gold. Slyly, he glanced at Marigold who seemed to be enjoying her bread and milk. This, he decided silently, could present a problem. He was hungry already; by dinnertime he would be famished. Unconsciously, he lifted his mug to his lips. As the hot liquid turned to molten gold, it burned his tongue and he cried out in pain.

"Oh, Father, have you burned yourself?" worried Marigold. She jumped from her chair and ran to her father's side.

"My dear daughter, my dear daughter!" The king leaned over and kissed her on the forehead. He watched with horror as she quickly changed from a lovely, bouncing little girl into a golden statue.

"What have I done? My precious daughter, what have I done?"

Midas sank into his chair and held his head in his hands. "Oh, wretched day! Oh, wretched king! Even the poorest swineherd in my kingdom is richer than I today."

And as he sat with tears streaming down his face, King Midas saw a glimmer of bright light and before him stood the stranger.

"Good day, King Midas," the stranger said. "Has the Golden Touch made you a happy man?"

"No, no! Never did I dream I could be so miserable! Would that I had never heard of the Golden Touch."

"But I thought that the Golden Touch was your heart's desire. Which would you rather have, the Golden Touch or a drink of cool water?"

The king clutched his parched throat. "A drink of cool water," he sighed longingly.

"Which would you rather have, the Golden Touch or your Marigold?"

"Oh, my darling daughter! If only I could hear her sweet voice again! I would not trade one of her dimples for all the gold in the world."

"You are a wiser man than you were yesterday, Midas. Very well," the stranger said thoughtfully, "if you would be free of the Golden Touch, plunge yourself into the stream at the end of the garden. Take with you a pitcher to fill with the water. Sprinkle each thing that you wish to return to its natural state."

And with that the stranger and the glowing light seemed to evaporate from the room.

Midas snatched a pitcher from the table, rushed to the stream, and dived in, shoes and all. Spluttering, he smiled as the golden pitcher regained its earthenware form.

He raced with the pitcher back to the castle and sprinkled the statue of his daughter. Slowly, her natural loveliness returned until only her brown curls retained a luster of golden highlights.

"Father, you are getting me all wet!" exclaimed Marigold.

The joyful king embraced his daughter exuberantly. "Come with me," he cried. He ran to the garden where he sprinkled the roses one by one, stopping now and again to smell the sweet fragrance or to marvel at the intricate beauty of the restored flowers.

Years later, when his grandchildren were at his knee, King Midas delighted in telling them the story of the Golden Touch. As an afterthought he would always add, "And now this is the only gold I care about at all." So saying, he would stroke affectionately the golden curls on each little head.

--Adapted for the flannel board

Trace the patterns and transfer them onto posterboard or heavy white paper. Color as desired and outline in black. Place each piece on the flannel board during the appropriate time in the story.

For special effects, make two sets of each of the properties that Midas turns to gold. Color one set in natural colors. Color the other set gold or glue on gold glitter. Place loops of removeable transparent tape on the backs of the gold pieces. As Midas touches each item, stick the gold counterpart on top of it. Remove the gold pieces as Midas sprinkles each with water.

Gold dust

Gold cup

Bag of Gold

King Midas

60

Rose bush

Marigold

Roses

61

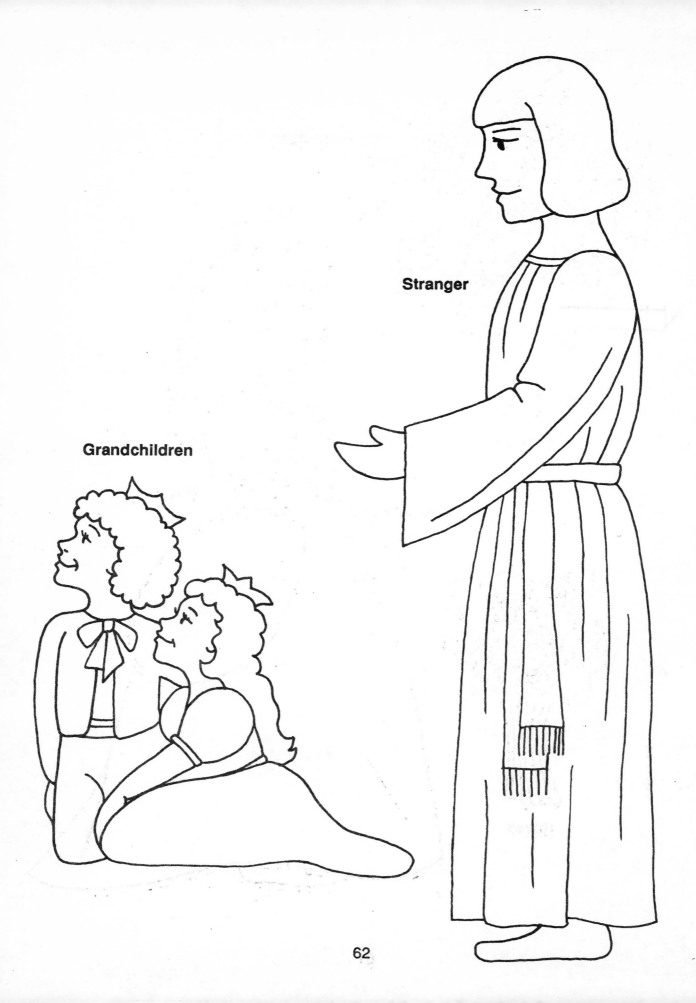

Stranger

Grandchildren

62

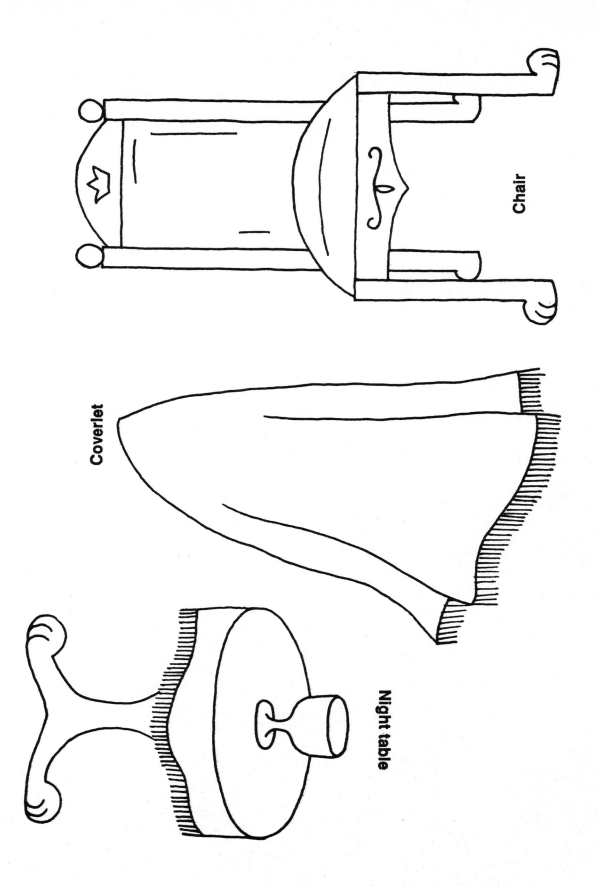

Chair

Coverlet

Night table

63

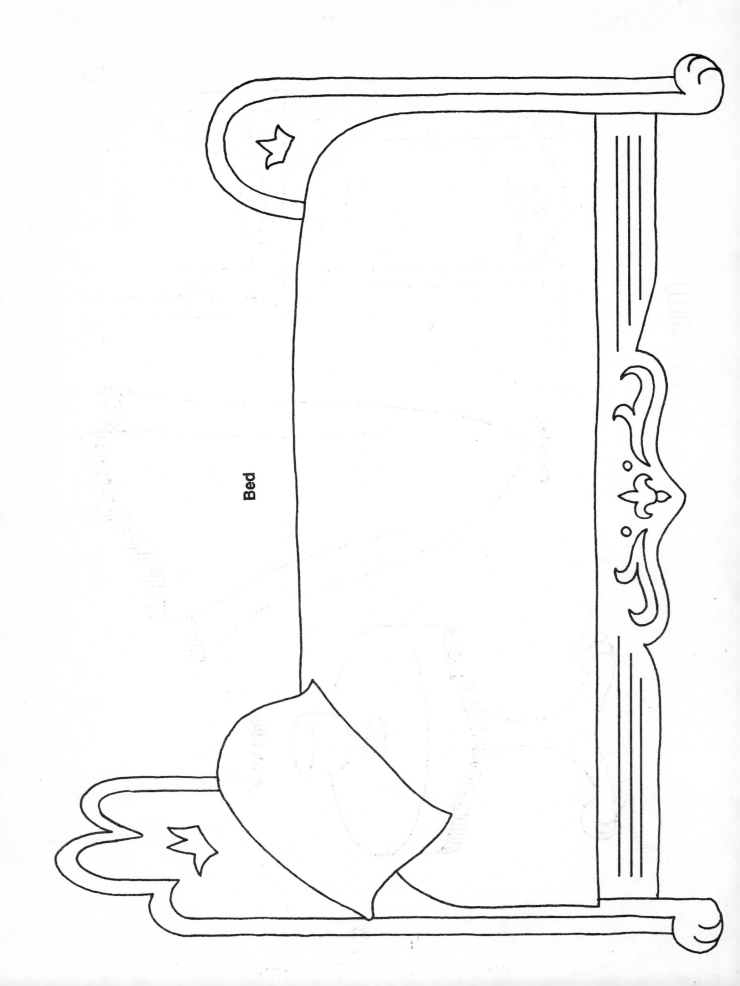

Bed

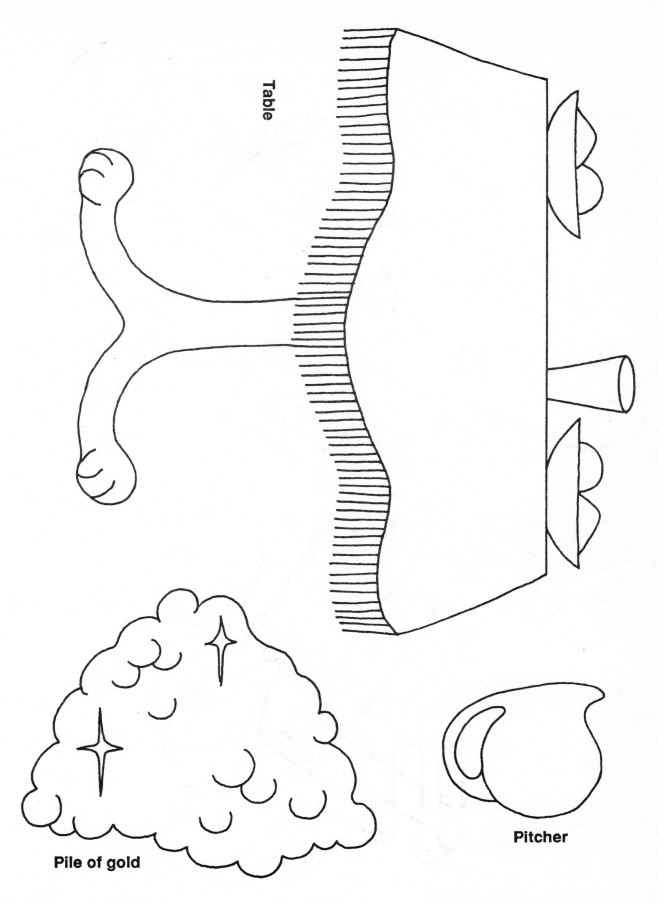

Table

Pile of gold

Pitcher

65

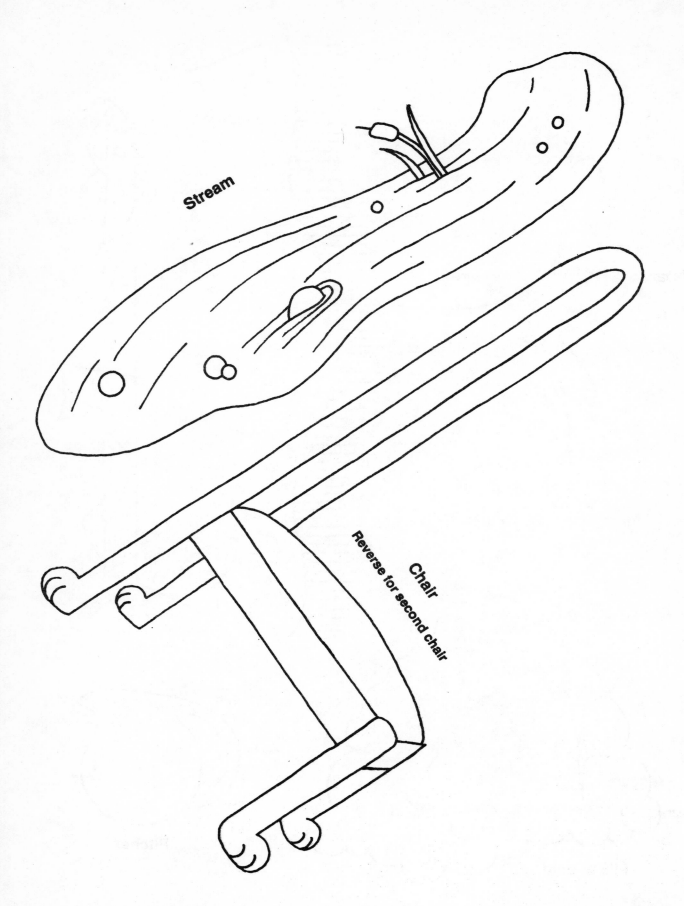

Stream

Chair
Reverse for second chair

66

THE TIGER, THE BRAHMAN, AND THE JACKAL

One day a brahman was walking through the jungle pondering good and evil when he came to a tiger struggling in a cage. The trapped tiger stamped and roared and bellowed his outrage. Upon seeing the brahman, he ceased roaring and began to plead. "Please, kind sir, please release me from this dreadful cage."

"What?" exclaimed the brahman, surprised at the tiger's change of temperament. "Why, you are indeed trapped in a cage."

The tiger asked again, "Please, holy one, please have mercy upon me and let me out of this cage."

The brahman looked at the tiger wisely. "I would not dare to free you," he said. "If I did, you would surely eat me."

"Eat you?" cried the tiger, "for letting me out of this cage? Of course, I would not eat you; I would be your slave."

The tiger and the brahman thus debated for some time. At last the kindly brahman felt sorry for the tiger and released him from the cage. At once the tiger pounced upon his benefactor. "You fool!" he said, "I shall eat you for my dinner. Surely you must know that I am half-starved

67

from my long entrapment."

Now it was the brahman's turn to beg for mercy. He pleaded so convincingly that the tiger was moved. "Very well," he said, "ask the first three things that you see whether I may justly eat you. I will abide by their decision. You must return here when the sun is high in the sky."

The brahman walked hopefully down the path until he came to a fig tree. To the fig tree he told his tale and asked if the tiger was justified in eating him.

"Ha!" sputtered the fig tree bitterly. "Why should you complain? All day long I provide shade for passers-by and instead of showing gratitude they tear off my branches. Don't whimper; accept your fate."

Somewhat shaken, the brahman continued on until he came to a water buffalo. Once again he told his story and posed his question.

The buffalo responded coldly to the brahman's plight. "You are truly a fool to expect gratitude. Look at me. When I give milk they feed me well, but now that I am dry, they give me only dry fodder."

The brahman was quite sad by now and trudged slowly down the path to where it joined the road. To the road he related his problem and begged for an opinion.

"How foolish you are to expect the tiger not to eat you!" said the road.

"All day long men walk on me and instead of showing me appreciation, they drop on me the ashes from their pipes and the husks from their grain."

Despairingly, the brahman turned back to face the tiger. On the way he met the jackal who called out, "What is the matter, brahman? You look as miserable as a fish out of water."

In detail the brahman explained to the jackal what had occurred.

"Oh, how confusing!" declared the jackal. "Would you mind telling me all of that again. It is all mixed up."

So the brahman told again of how he had freed the tiger from a cage and how the tiger planned to break his promise and eat the holy man for his dinner.

The jackal shook his head. "Oh, dear, I don't understand in the least. Let's go back to the place where it all happened and perhaps then I can understand it."

The brahman and the jackal walked back down the path to where the tiger waited by the cage, pacing up and down impatiently.

"You have certainly kept me waiting long enough. Come, let us get on with our dinner," snarled the tiger.

"Please, lord tiger," begged the brahman, "just allow me a few more moments for I am trying to explain things to this slow-witted jackal."

"Very well," the tiger agreed, "five minutes and absolutely no more."

So the brahman began again. "You see, jackal, the tiger was in that cage. He promised me that he would not eat me if I let him out. So I let him out and now he is planning to eat me."

The jackal looked confused. "Oh, my poor, poor brain," he said. "Let me see...how did it all begin? You were in the cage and the tiger came walking by..."

"What a fool!" exclaimed the impatient tiger. "It was I that was in the cage."

The jackal smiled with relief. "Of course. It was I who was in the cage...oh, no, I was not in the cage. What is wrong with me? Let's see...the tiger was in the brahman and the cage came walking by...no, no, that cannot be right either. Oh, dear, I am all muddled. Go ahead with dinner; I'll never understand anyway."

"You will, too, understand!" the angry tiger shouted. "I will make you understand. You look here. I am the tiger, agreed?"

"Yes, lord tiger."

"And that is the brahman."

"Yes, lord tiger."

"And I was in this cage. Do you understand me?"

Once more the jackal looked puzzled. "Yes, I-er-I, no, please, lord tiger, I don't understand."

"What don't you understand?" snarled the tiger.

"I don't understand how you got into the cage."

"I got into the cage the usual way, of course."

The jackal covered his eyes with his paws and said, "Oh, my poor confused brain is spinning. Please do not get angry, lord tiger, but what is the usual way?"

The tiger stared at the jackal in disbelief, his patience nearly at an end. "You slow-witted jackal," he roared, "this is the usual way." He stomped angrily into the cage. "Now do you understand?"

"Perfectly!" The jackal smiled as he locked the cage. "And as far as I am concerned, this is the way that things will remain. Come, holy brahman, let us leave this ungrateful beast to his just desert."

And each went his separate way into the jungle.

--Adapted for the flannel board

Trace the patterns and transfer them onto posterboard. Or perhaps, because of the detail in the pictures, you might prefer to copy the pages on a copier and attach them to posterboard. Color as desired. The jungle foliage can be placed on opposite ends of the flannel board to serve as a frame for each scene. Use each picture for the appropriate scene in the story.

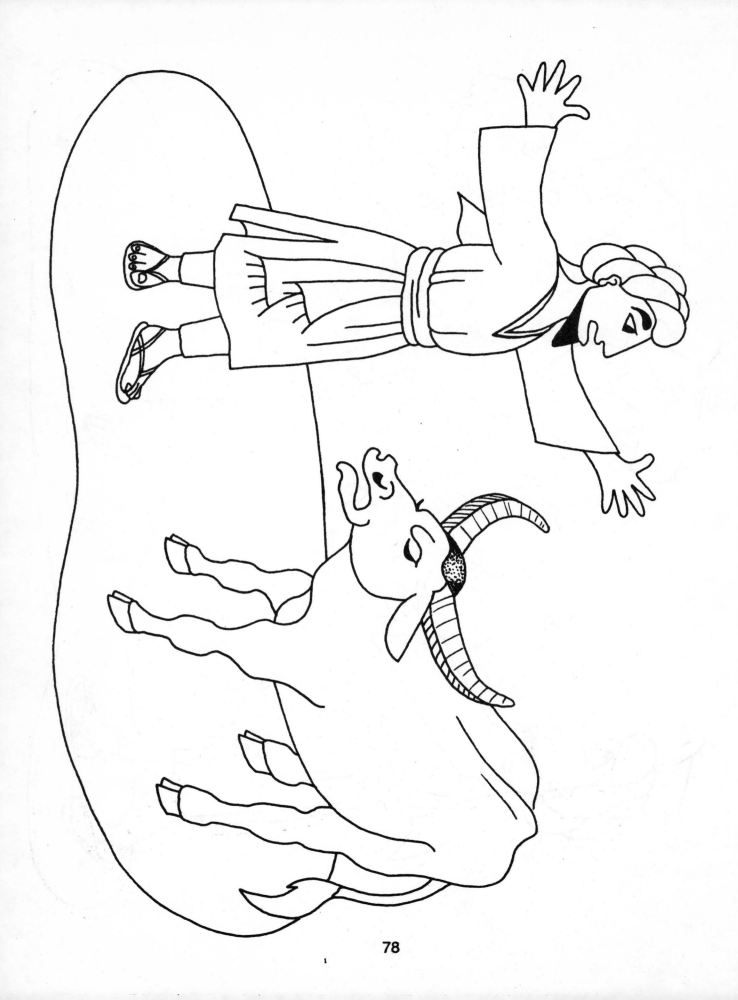

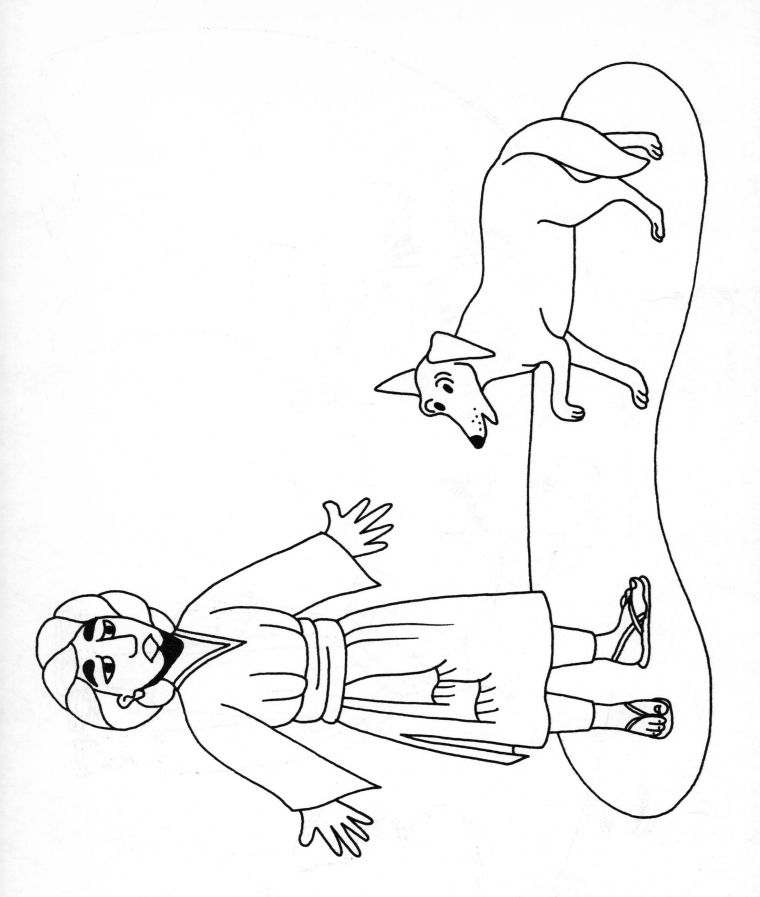

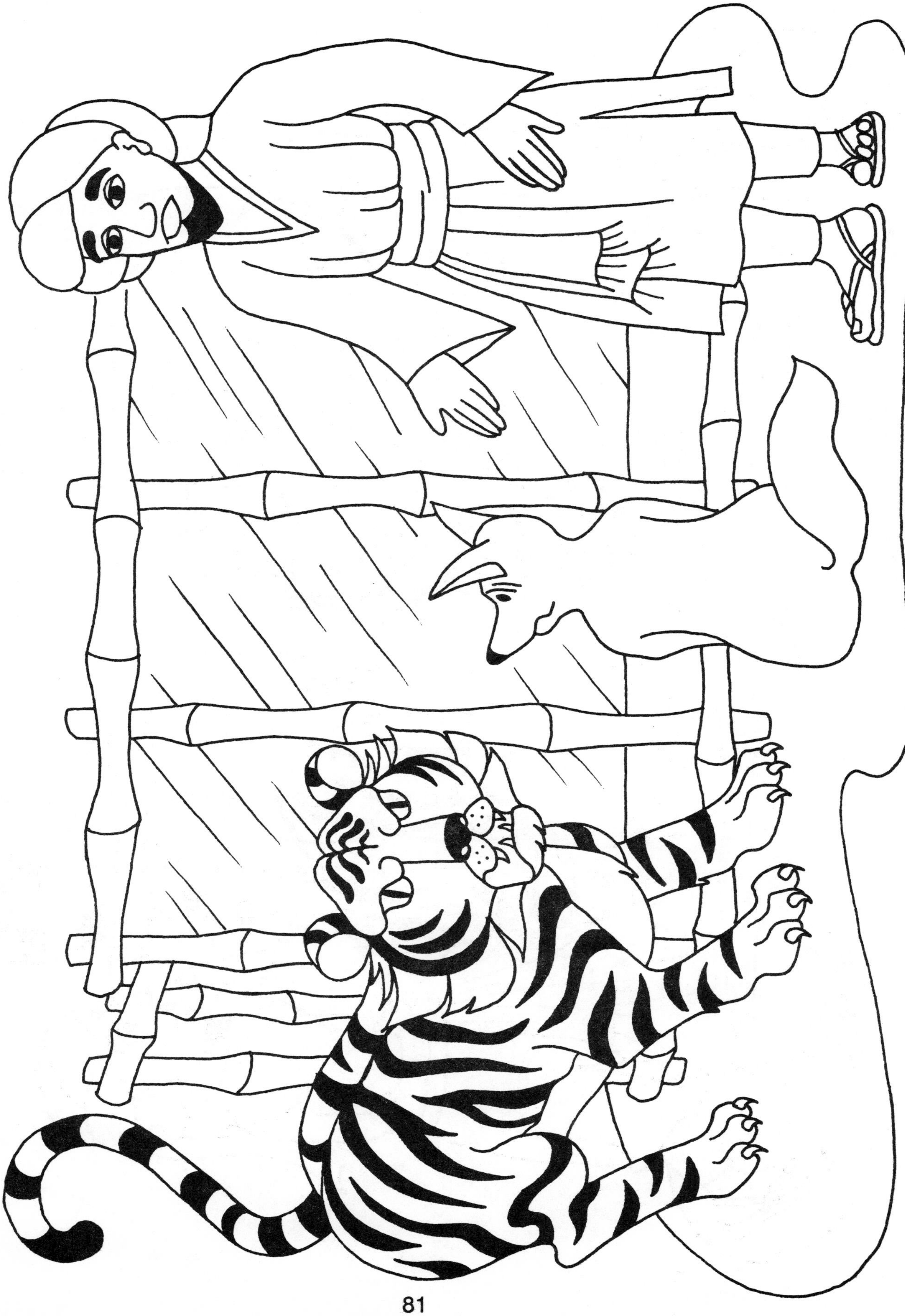

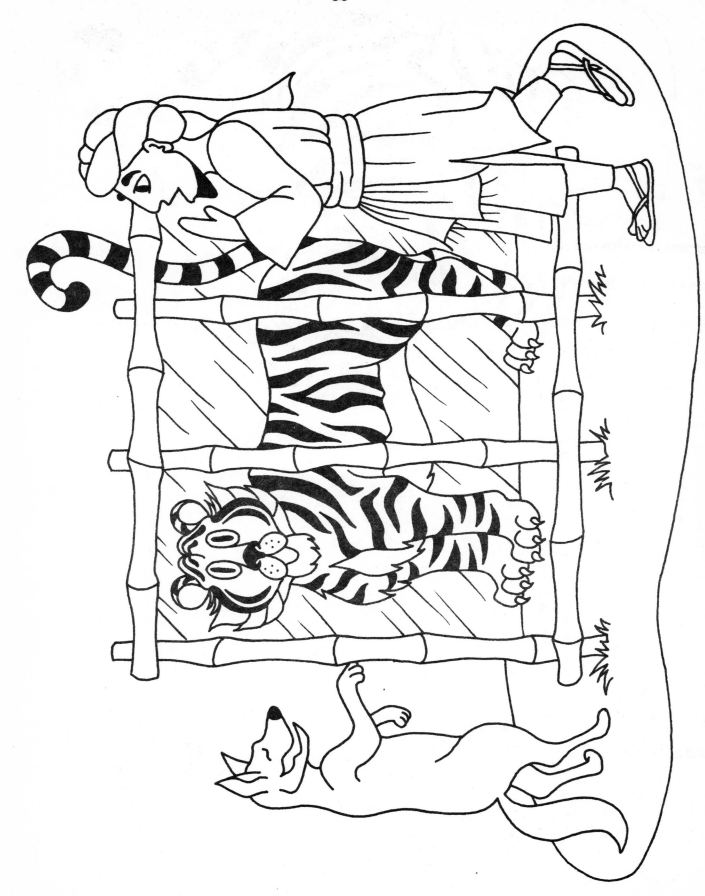

PARTICIPATION ACTIVITIES

Should children participate actively in story programs? It depends entirely on the personal choice of the story teller and on the type of story program being presented. Most older children enjoy engaging in some part of the program, just as preschoolers like fingerplays and action rhymes. Included in this section are a variety of participation activities, i.e., rounds, choral readings, and dramatic interpretations.

Singing in rounds is easy and fun. To introduce rounds, you may want to begin with an old favorite, such as *Frere Jacques* or *Row, Row, Row Your Boat*. Follow the old stand-by with a new round related to your program theme. Teach the words, next the tune, and next the song in unison. Finally, try singing the round in two or three parts.

In using choral readings in your story program, you should either provide hand-out sheets with the verses printed on them or, preferably, use an overhead projector so that you can be sure that the children are all following your directions. Since few children will have experience with choral reading, you will probably want to begin with simple unison reading, e.g., *If You Should Meet a Crocodile* or *The Man in the Moon*.

From there you may progress to groups-in-turn, e.g., **Solomon Grundy**. More complex forms include solo-and-group, e.g., **Hector Protector**, cumulative groups, e.g., **For Want of a Nail**, and alternating groups and solos, e.g., **Paul Bunyan**.

After the children are accustomed to participating in your story program, you may wish to introduce some dramatic activities. Begin simply, with perhaps **A Was an Apple Pie**, in which the action is specifically indicated. Follow this verse with something such as **Three Little Mice** which can be pantomimed. Now try a selection, perhaps **The North Wind and the Sun**, requiring a bit more creative interpretation. Finally, attempt some higher level of dramatic activity. Remind the children that there is no right or wrong way to interpret a story or an action. Encourage them to think creatively and to respond positively to the work of their peers.

IF YOU SHOULD MEET A CROCODILE

Unison: If you should meet a Crocodile,

Don't take a stick and poke him;

Ignore the welcome in his smile,

Be careful not to stroke him.

For as he sleeps upon the Nile,

He thinner gets and thinner;

And whene'er you meet a Crocodile,

He's ready for his dinner.

--Author Unknown

CHORAL READING

THE MAN IN THE MOON

Unison: The Man in the Moon as he sails the sky

Is a very remarkable skipper,

But he made a mistake when he tried to take

A drink of milk from the Dipper.

He dipped right out of the Milky Way,

And slowly and carefully filled it,

The Big Bear growled, and the Little Bear howled

And frightened him so that he spilled it.

--Old Rhyme

CHORAL READING

MILKWEED SEEDS

Unison: In a milkweed cradle,

Snug and warm,

Baby seeds are hiding,

Safe from harm.

Open wide the cradle,

Hold it high!

Come, Mr. Wind!

Help them fly.

--Unknown

CHORAL READING

SOLOMON GRUNDY

Group 1:   Solomon Grundy

Group 2:   Born on Monday,

Group 3:   Christened on Tuesday,

Group 4:   Married on Wednesday,

Group 5:   Took ill on Thursday,

Group 6:   Worse on Friday,

Group 7:   Died on Saturday,

Group 8:   Buried on Sunday.

All: This is the end of Solomon Grundy.

--Nursery Rhyme

CHORAL READING

HECTOR PROTECTOR

Group 1:   Hector Protector was dressed all in green;

Group 2:   Hector Protector was sent to the Queen.

Solo 1:   The Queen did not like him,

Solo 2: No more did the King;

All: So Hector Protector was sent back again.

--Nursery Rhyme

CHORAL READING

FOR WANT OF A NAIL

Group 1: For want of a nail, the shoe was lost,

Groups 1-2: For want of a shoe, the horse was lost,

Groups 1-3: For want of a horse, the rider was lost.

Groups 1-4: For want of a rider, the battle was lost.

Groups 1-5: For want of a battle, the kingdom was lost,

All: And all for the want of a horseshoe nail.

--Nursery Rhyme

CHORAL READING

WHERE ARE YOU GOING, MY PRETTY MAID?

Boys: Where are you going to, my pretty maid?

Girls: I'm going a'milking, sir, she said.

Boys: May I go with you, my pretty maid?

Girls: You're kindly welcome, sir, she said.

Boys: Say, will you marry me, my pretty maid?

Girls: Yes, if you please, kind sir, she said.

Boys: What is your father, my pretty maid?

Girls: My father's a farmer, sir, she said.

Boys: What is your fortune, my pretty maid?

Girls: My face is my fortune, sir, she said.

Boys: Then I can't marry you, my pretty maid.

Girls: Nobody asked you, sir, she said.

--Nursery Rhyme

THE PUZZLED CENTIPEDE

All:	A centipede was happy quite,
	Until a frog in fun
	Said,
Solo:	"Pray which leg comes after which?"
Group 1:	This raised her mind to such a pitch,
Group 2:	She lay distracted in the ditch
All:	Considering how to run.

--Unknown

CHORAL READING

MR. NOBODY

Group 1:	I know a funny little man,
	As quiet as a mouse,
Group 2:	Who does the mischief that is done
	In everybody's house!
Group 3:	There's no one ever sees his face,

And yet we all agree

All: That every plate we break was cracked

By Mr. Nobody.

Group 1:   'Tis he who always tears our books,

Who leaves the doors ajar,

Group 2:   He pulls the buttons from our shirts,

And scatters pins afar;

Group 3:   That squeaking door will always squeak,

For , prithee, don't you see,

All: We leave the oiling to be done

By Mr. Nobody.

Group 1:   He puts damp wood upon the fire,

That kettles cannot boil;

Group 2:   His are the feet that bring in mud,

And all the carpets soil.

The papers always are mislaid,

Who had them last but he?

There's no one tosses them about

But Mr. Nobody.

Group 3:   The finger marks upon the door

            By none of us are made;

Group 1:   We never leave the blinds unclosed,

            To let the curtains fade.

Group 2:   The ink we never spill; the boots

            That lying round you see

Group 3:   Are not our boots;--they all belong

All: To Mr. Nobody.

                                    --Unknown

CHORAL READING

JOHNNY APPLESEED

All: Goin' West?

Solo 1:   I'm a'goin' 'cause I'm Appleseed John.

Solo 2:   Folks are a-trav'lin'; they're a-movin' on.

Solo 3:   But they've got no apple trees to take along.

All: So I'm walkin' and I'm plantin' apples.

            Appleseed John.

Solo 4:	Just me and my Bible and my apple seeds--
Solo 5:	That's all I've got with me 'cause I've got few needs.
Solo 6:	And plantin' those apples are my only deeds
All:	While I'm walkin' and a-plantin' apples.
	Johnny Appleseed.
Solo 7:	I planted apples clear to Or-e-gon;
Solo 8:	I tended the trees, then I traveled on,
Solo 9:	So folks have found apples wherever they've gone.
All:	Thanks for walkin', thanks for plantin' apples.
	Appleseed John.

CHORAL READING

PAUL BUNYAN

Groups 1-2:	Paul was born with a long curly beard.
Group 3:	There wasn't a thing of which he was afeared.
Child 1:	The strangest tales that I ever heared was of
All:	Paul Bunyan.

Child 2:	He strode through the woods with his mighty ax.
Child 3:	He could chop down a tree with a couple of whacks.
Child 1:	Weren't no man big enough to foller his tracks.
All:	Paul Bunyan.
Group 1:	He had a big ox that was blue as the sky.
Group 2:	Those two hauled logs loaded mountaintop-high.
Group 3:	They could clear a whole timber in a day, should they try.
All:	Paul Bunyan.
Child 4:	Ole Paul and Babe changed the whole terrain.
Group 1:	They straightened out a river with a great big chain.
Groups 2-3:	They cleared North Dakota for a fine farming plain.
All:	Paul Bunyan.
All:	Whenever Paul Bunyan and Babe would appear,
	The lumberjacks would holler and raise up a cheer,
Child 5:	And tell all the tales you would want to hear of
All:	Paul Bunyan.

PARTICIPATION ACTIVITY -- ROUNDS

KOOKABURRA

Kookaburra sits in the old gum tree,

Merry, merry king of the bush is he.

Laugh! Kookaburra, laugh!

Kookaburra, gay your life must be.

--Traditional

SWEETLY SINGS THE DONKEY

Sweetly sings the donkey at the break of day.

If you do not feed him, this is what he'll say:

Hee-haw, hee-haw, hee-haw, hee-haw, hee-haw.

--Traditional

PARTICIPATION ACTIVITY -- ROUNDS

THE GHOST OF JOHN

Have you seen the ghost of John?
Long white bones and the rest all gone,
Oooh----oooh

Wouldn't it be chilly with no skin on?

--Traditional

Piano Accompaniment

A WAS AN APPLE PIE

A was an apple pie;

B bit it,

C cut it,

D dealt it,

E eat it,

F fought for it,

G got it,

H had it,

I inspected it,

J jumped for it,

K kept it,

L longed for it,

M mourned for it,

N nodded at it,

O opened it,

P peeped in it,

Q quartered it,

R ran for it,

S stole it,

T took it,

U upset it,

V viewed it,

W wanted it,

X, Y, Z and ampersand

All wished for a piece in hand.

--Nursery Rhyme

This verse is a good introduction to dramatic activities. Read the verse aloud. Then re-read, allowing time for the children to dramatize each line. Even the most reluctant participants will become involved before you come to the end of the alphabet.

DRAMATIC ACTIVITY

THREE LITTLE MICE

Three little mice sat down to spin;

Pussy came by, and she peeked in;

"What are you doing, my little men?"

"We're making coats for gentlemen."

"May I come in and bite off your threads?"

"No, no, Miss Pussy! You'll bite off our heads!"

"Oh, no, I'll not, I'll help you to spin."

"That may be so, but you can't come in."

--Nursery Rhyme

This short narrative verse is a good selection for beginners. Ask one child to be the cat and the rest the mice. Read the rhyme and allow the children to interpret it in pantomime. After they are familiar with it, let them speak the dialogue while they are dramatizing the action.

THE QUARRELSOME KITTENS

Two little kittens, one stormy night,

Began to quarrel, and then to fight.

One had a mouse, and the other had none,

And that's the way the quarrel begun.

"I'll have that mouse," said the bigger cat,

"You'll have that mouse? We'll see about that!"

"I WILL have that mouse," said the older one,

"You SHAN'T have the mouse," said the little one.

I told you before 'twas a stormy night,

When these two little kittens began to fight.

The old woman seized her sweeping broom,

And swept the two kittens right out of the room.

The ground was all covered with frost and snow,

And the two little kittens had nowhere to go.

So they laid them down on the mat at the door,

While the old woman finished sweeping the floor.

Then they crept in as quiet as mice,

All wet with snow, and as cold as ice.

For they found it much better, that stormy night,

To lie down and sleep, than to quarrel and fight.

--Old Rhyme

Read the verse aloud. Re-read the verse stanza by stanza, pausing
after each so that the children can act it out.

DRAMATIC ACTIVITY

THE NORTH WIND AND THE SUN

The North Wind and the Sun were having an argument: each believed himself to be the stronger. Neither could convince the other that he was right.

Just then both saw a lone traveler walking down the road. Here was the perfect test, they both agreed; whichever one got the traveler's coat off first would be the winner.

The North Wind tried first. In his fiercest manner he blew gust after gust of strong winds at the man. To his dismay the man pulled his coat tighter around himself for protection from the blasts of cold wind.

Then the Sun took his turn. Gently and cheerfully, he focused his warm beams on the traveler. Soon the man slowed his pace, then he wiped perspiration from his brow, and finally, he removed his coat and sat down in the shade to rest and cool off. And so the Sun was declared winner of the argument.

MORAL: Gentleness may succeed where force has failed.

*--Retold from LaFontaine's **Fables***

Read the story aloud to the group. Select children to represent the three characters. Read the story again as the children pantomime the action. Now try letting the children mime the story without benefit of the spoken word.

DRAMATIC ACTIVITY

THE TOWN MOUSE
AND
THE COUNTRY MOUSE

Once upon a time a mouse lived in a house in the country. Although he liked his little abode, he sometimes felt that life was hard. Food was not always easy to come by, and many nights he went to sleep with an empty stomach. Even so, he slept soundly, dreaming of the simple fare that he was sure to find next day to satisfy his hunger.

One day the country mouse received a message that his cousin, who dwelt in the nearby town, was coming to visit. He was delighted and scurried about, collecting a corn kernel here, a wheat grain there, stocking his larder with the best he could find.

On the appointed day the town mouse arrived.

"Welcome, Cousin," exclaimed the country mouse. "I am pleased to share my humble home with you."

All went well for a day or two. At last the town mouse could no longer contain himself.

"Cousin," he said, "how can you bear to live thus isolated in the country? And how can you tolerate this meager pauper's menu which you daily endure?"

And so he railed and ranted until the country mouse was truly dissatisfied with his existence.

"Come back to town with me, Cousin," the town mouse suggested grandly. "I shall introduce you to properly elegant dining."

At first the country mouse resisted, but at last he agreed to accompany his cousin back to town.

When they arrived at the home of the town mouse, the country cousin was wide-eyed, staring at first this, then that.

"Oh, Cousin," he cried, "I never imagined such riches! Why, oh, why, did I stay so long in the country."

"This is nothing!" The town mouse waved aside all his cousin's exclamations of wonder. "Come with me to the dining room. I will show you cuisine suitable for a mouse's palate."

So they proceeded until he came to a huge table, and following his town cousin, the country mouse scampered up to the table top. What an awesome sight! A plate of fine Gruyere cheese sat on one corner of the table. An exquisitely decorated cake sat on another. The country mouse grabbed crumbs and began stuffing them into his mouth.

"No crumbs for us, my cousin," proclaimed the town mouse. "Would you please join me in having a bit of cheese?"

Suddenly the table shook and the air was rent with hisses and growls.

"Run! Run for your life!" screamed the town mouse as he led the way toward a small hole in the wall.

Inside the hole the cousins stood trembling and shaking while outside the hole a furry paw pounded on the wall.

The country mouse panted breathlessly, "What was that monster that nearly devoured us?"

Said the town mouse, "That was only the cat who earns his keep by chasing mice. It's the small price we pay for such fine food."

"Such a small price is too costly for me," replied the country mouse. "Tomorrow I shall return to the safety of my own home. I would rather eat simple, plain fare in peace and tranquility than a king's portion in fear and trembling."

And the very next day he returned to his home in the country.

--Adapted from Aesop's **Fables**

Read the fable aloud to the group. Instead of dramatizing the story, ask the children to try to interpret each mouse's thoughts, feelings, and attitudes by facial expressions and body language. Perhaps you might try some of the following suggestions.

How does the country mouse hunt for food? How does he sleep? How does he react to the news that his cousin is coming to visit? What does the town mouse feel when he eats the corn and wheat? How does he look when he is scorning life in the country? How does he invite his cousin to visit in town? How does the country mouse look when he enters the town? How does he look when he arrives on top of the table? How do the mice react when they see the cat? Demonstrate their relief when they are safely inside the hole. How does the country mouse appear when he resolves to return home?

After trying to express some of these feelings, the children may want to discuss and analyze which expressions were most successful and why. Remind them, however, that all interpretations are correct -- each reflects the individuality of the child and is, therefore, acceptable.

WHY THE ROBIN'S BREAST IS RED

Long ago in the far, cold North where the ice never melts, a hunter and his small son lived alone. Dressed head to toe in furs, they were snug inside their icy igloo. They were snug, however, only because of the fire that burned at their threshold. Both man and boy worked hard keeping the fire burning brightly; both knew that were it to die, they too would die soon after.

In all the Northland they had one living enemy: the great white bear, whom they hunted. The bear, too, knew that man and boy would die without the fire and he longed to put it out. Only fear of the hunter's arrows kept him grumbling just out of range.

One day the hunter fell ill and could no longer hunt nor guard the fire. Night and day the boy tended the fire, straining against fatigue and hunger. He watched fearfully as the pile of sticks and twigs grew smaller, but he was reluctant to leave the fire untended while he gathered more.

At last the boy was overcome by fatigue. Despite his efforts his eyelids closed, his head nodded with drowsiness, and he was soon sound asleep.

The great white bear had been drawing nearer and nearer. Seeing the boy asleep, he knew that his chance had finally come. He lumbered silently to the fire and tramped out the flames. When all that remained was gray ash, the bear sauntered away, confident that he would no longer be bothered by the hunter.

The sleeping boy failed to notice that the fire had gone out. Neither he nor his ailing father stirred as the deadly cold settled around them. Only the small brown robin saw what the bear had done.

The robin rushed to the heap of ashes. He scratched and scraped through them, searching for a spark. At last he found a tiny live coal which he fanned with his wings for a long time. The coal glowed brighter and broke into a tiny flame. Still the robin fanned although the flame made him hot and, indeed, scorched the feathers on his breast quite red.

The flame grew, but still the robin fanned. When the robin was nearly faint from the heat, the boy roused in his sleep and jumped up to feed the flickering flame.

At that moment the hunter, too, roused himself, and feeling much better, smiled at his busy son.

Neither man nor boy ever knew they were saved from certain death by the robin. As for the robin, to this day he has always had a red breast.

--A traditional Eskimo legend

Tell the story or read it aloud to the group. Ask the children to think about the dreary cold and the necessity for the hunter and the boy to keep the fire burning. Assign children to be the four major characters. Read or tell the legend again, letting the children dramatize the action.

PUPPETS IN THE STORY PROGRAM

Puppets enhance a story program and are ever popular with children of all ages. Included in this section are a variety of puppet activities, ranging from a simple lap puppet story to a relatively complex stage drama. All, however, are designed for one to three puppeteers and all are simple to prepare from inexpensive materials.

The Deaf Woman's Courtship, an old folk song which appeals to the sense of humor of older children, utilizes styrofoam ball hand puppets to be operated by the leader or by two of the participants. *The Hoca's Three Sermons* also uses a styrofoam ball hand puppet which appears from and disappears into a box held on the lap of the storyteller. *The Hare and the Hedgehog* is performed on stage with large, double-sided stick puppets. *The Bear Says North* is also performed on stage with paper bag puppets. *The Miller, the Boy, and the Donkey* is a shadow puppet tableau; it is extremely effective but requires two puppeteers and a technical assistant. The most complicated of the puppet activities is *The Sorcerer's Apprentice*. Using both hand puppets and stick puppets, it necessitates much practice and careful timing to achieve a polished performance.

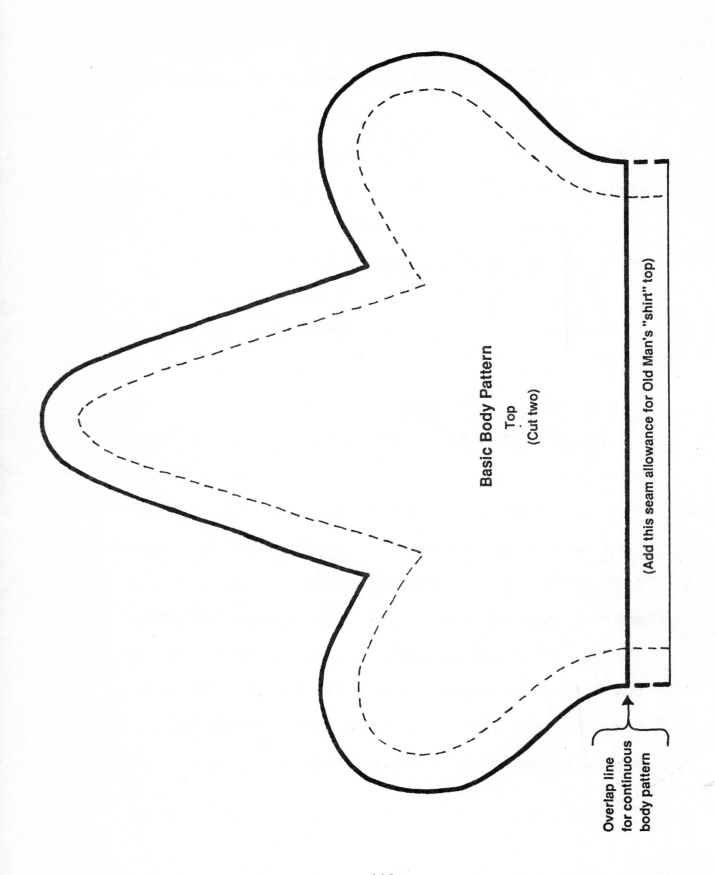

Basic Body Pattern

Top

(Cut two)

(Add this seam allowance for Old Man's "shirt" top)

Overlap line
for continuous
body pattern

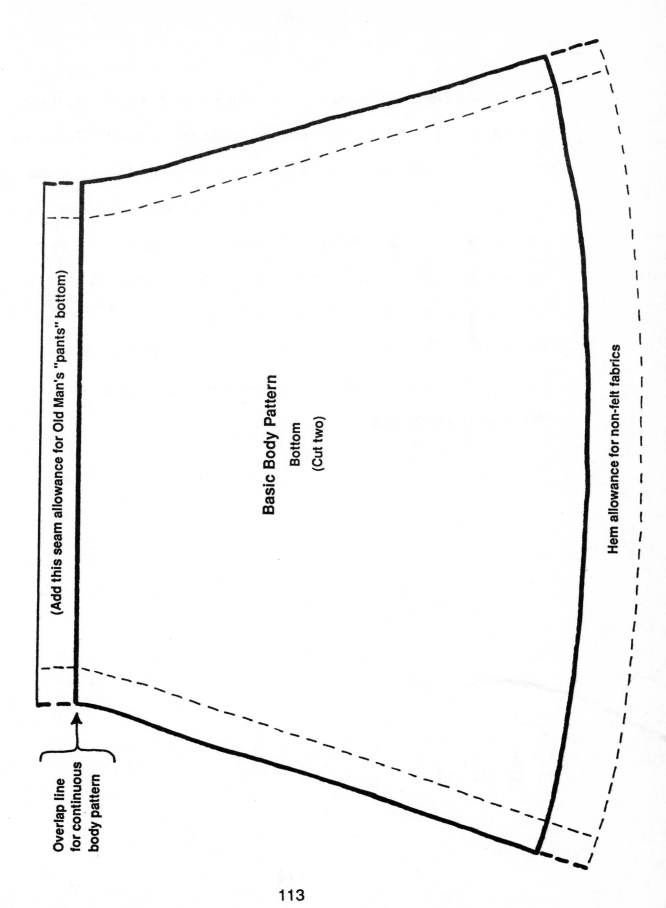

(Add this seam allowance for Old Man's "pants" bottom)

Basic Body Pattern

Bottom

(Cut two)

Hem allowance for non-felt fabrics

Overlap line
for continuous
body pattern

When you are operating puppets, remember that all movements must be exaggerated in order that the audience grasp their intention. Be sure that the only puppet moving on stage is the one that is talking; it is the main cue that viewers can follow. Practice manipulating your puppet in front of the mirror. Is it accurately interpreting the story? If not, try changing the motions to be more effective. When you are practicing a puppet play to be performed on stage, arrange for a "director" to sit in front of the stage and correct your animation. The director can see what you cannot and can assist you in giving your production a more professional appearance.

PUPPET/PARTICIPATION SONG

DEAF WOMAN'S COURTSHIP

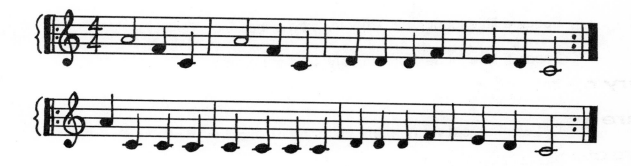

Old woman, old woman, will you do my shearing?

Old woman, old woman, will you do my shearing?

Speak a little louder, sir, I'm very hard of hearing.

Speak a little louder, sir, I'm very hard of hearing.

Old woman, old woman, will you do my carding?

Old woman, old woman, will you do my carding?

Speak a little louder, sir, I'm very hard of hearing.

Speak a little louder, sir, I'm very hard of hearing.

Old woman, old woman, are you good at spinning?

Old woman, old woman, are you good at spinning?

Speak a little louder, sir, I'm very hard of hearing.

Speak a little louder, sir, I'm very hard of hearing.

Old woman, old woman, are you fond of weaving?

Old woman, old woman, are you fond of weaving?

Speak a little louder, sir, I'm very hard of hearing.

Speak a little louder, sir, I'm very hard of hearing.

Old woman, old woman, will you let me court you?

Old woman, old woman, will you let me court you?

Speak a little louder, sir, I think I almost hear you.

Speak a little louder, sir, I think I almost hear you.

Old woman, old woman, why don't we get married?

Old woman, old woman, why don't we get married?

Lawsy-mercy on my soul, now I hear you clearly!

Lawsy-mercy on my soul, now I hear you clearly!

--Traditional song with puppets

To involve the children actively in this song, divide the group into two parts, allowing the boys to sing the old man's lines and the girls to sing the old woman's lines. Have the boys begin the song very loudly, diminishing slightly on each verse until they are barely whispering the last stanza. If you prefer, ask the children to dramatize the song. It may be necessary for you to explain some of the unfamiliar terms before you begin this activity.

As a variation the song can be dramatized by using styrofoam ball hand puppets made from the patterns included on the following pages. To make the Old Woman and Old Man puppets, use the following directions.

1. For the heads use 2 1/2" styrofoam balls. Carve a hole in the bottom of each to fit finger. Glue hair and features to faces as shown in drawings. Use gray yarn for hair, eyebrows, beard, and moustache. Beard is made of lengths of yarn folded in half with folded end only glued to face, leaving cut ends to hang free.

Old Man

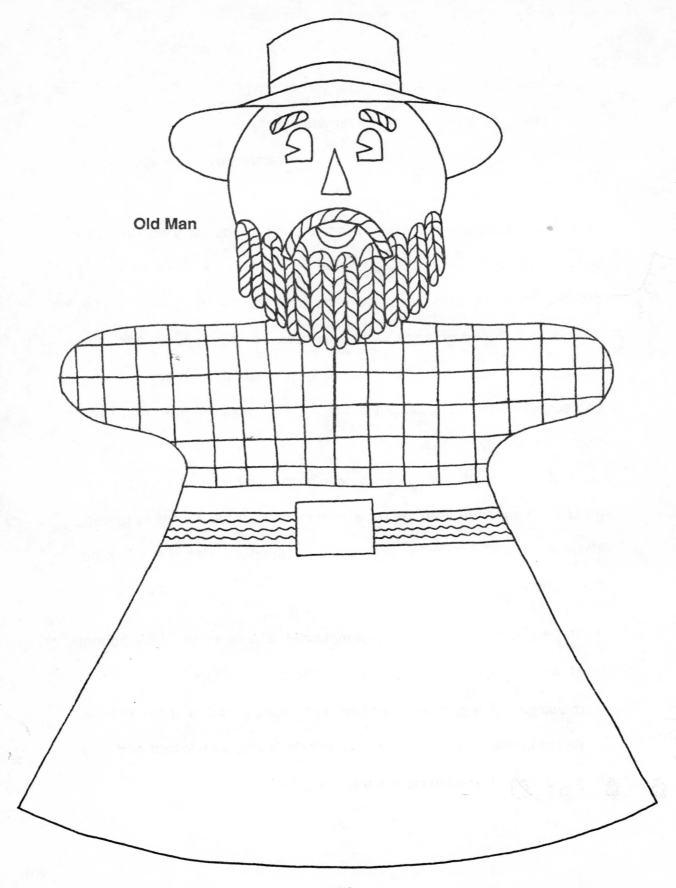

Old Woman

119

2. For the dust bonnet cut circle pattern out of small-print fabric used for body pattern. Using 2 yards of 3/8" lace, place wrong side of lace facing right side of fabric, and scalloped edge facing towards center of circle. Stitch straight edge of lace 1/2" from edge of circle as shown on pattern piece. Press under overhanging fabric to wrong side. Stitch just above original stitch line. Trim excess if necessary. Using doubled matching thread, baste 1/4" from top of lace using small stitches. Pull thread until hat is correct size for head. Secure ends. Stuff hat loosely and glue to head. Use short straight pins (sequin pins) to secure if necessary.

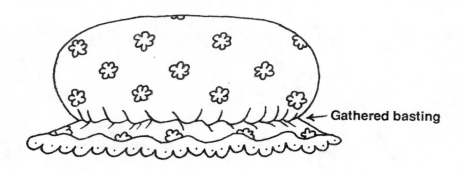

← Gathered basting

3. For the Old Woman's body use the continuous body pattern; cut pattern pieces out of small-print fabric used for bonnet. Add hem allowance for non-felt fabrics. For blouse front cut two pieces of lace,

3" long each. On right side of body front, place straight edges of lace 5/8" apart centered lengthwise with ends starting even with top corners of arms where they meet the neck. Stitch.

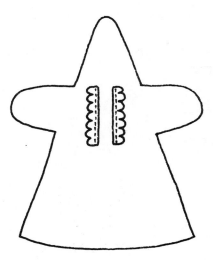

For collar cut one piece of lace 3 1/4" long. Stitch horizontally to overlap tops of blouse front lace.

For the apron cut out pattern piece of contrasting felt. Center short edge (top) of apron on 6" piece of lace matching straight edges. Stitch. Sew 5" piece of lace to apron bottom turning under ends of lace to back. Center apron on front of dress, overlapping top of apron and blouse front lace, even with bottom corners of arms. Stitch across straight edge of apron top lace only, leaving rest of apron to hang free.

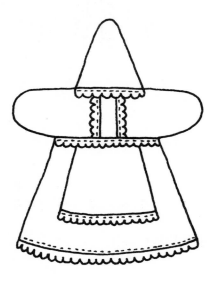

For back cut piece of lace 6" long. Sew to right side of back, even with bottom corners of arms. With right sides together stitch front and back dress pieces together 3/8" from edge leaving bottom open. Clip curves. Turn. With wrong side of lace facing right side of fabric and scalloped edge facing up towards apron, stitch straight edge of lace

1/2" from bottom edge of dress bottom. Press under overhanging

fabric to wrong side. Sew just above original stitch line. Tie bow

from 12" piece of lace. Sew to center of back lace for apron bow.

Glue 3 small felt circles to blouse front for buttons. NOTE: If dress

fabric is thin, slip cardboard inside before gluing.

4. To make the Old Man's hat cut two strips of felt 3/8" x 2 3/4" for the

crown. Criss cross over small circle cut from center of hat brim felt.

Glue and let dry thoroughly.

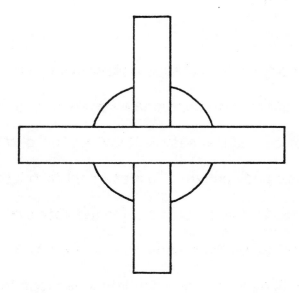

Cut top of hat from poster board. Score along line with a ball point pen.

Clip to score line where shown. Fold clipped ends to right angle.

Overlap 3/8" on each end and tape forming tube as shown.

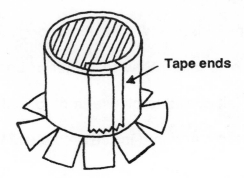

Tape ends

Slip felt hat brim over tube. Glue to clipped edges of tube. Cut strip of hat felt 4 1/2" x 3/8". Glue to hat for hat band. Using a sharp knife, shave crown of head flat. Position hat and glue. Use short pins to secure if necessary.

5. The puppet body of the Old Man is designed to simulate a "shirt" top and "pants" bottom. Use appropriate fabrics for this appearance. Cut out pattern pieces adding seam allowances for "shirt" and "pants" as shown on basic body pattern. To make front, with right sides together stitch "shirt" top to "pants" bottom. On the right side of "pants" front, sew braid 3/8" down from seam line to form belt. To make back repeat instructions for front. With right sides together, stitch front to back leaving bottom open. Clip curves. Turn. Hem bottom edge. Glue gold or yellow felt rectangle to center front of belt for buckle.

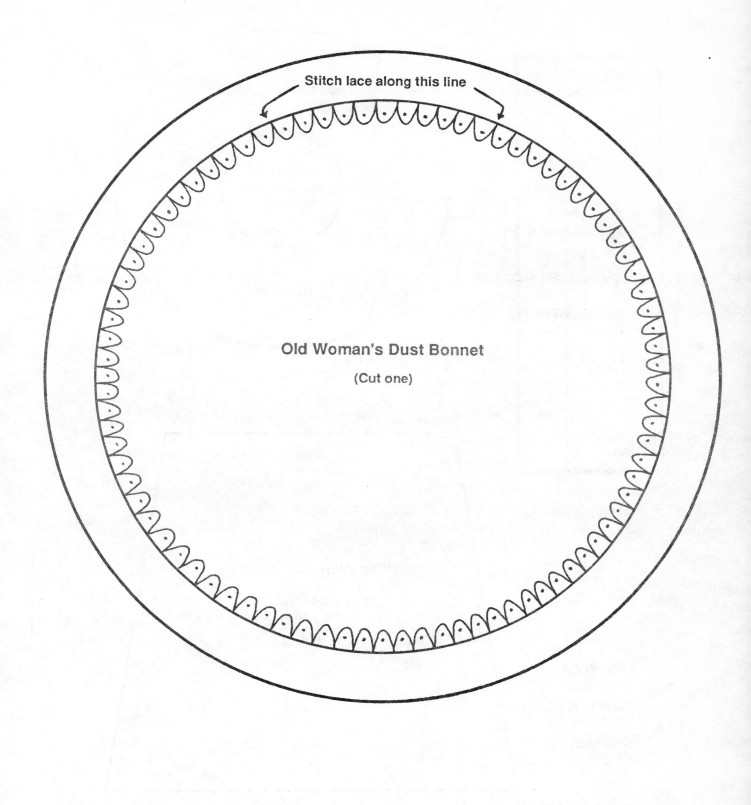

Stitch lace along this line

Old Woman's Dust Bonnet

(Cut one)

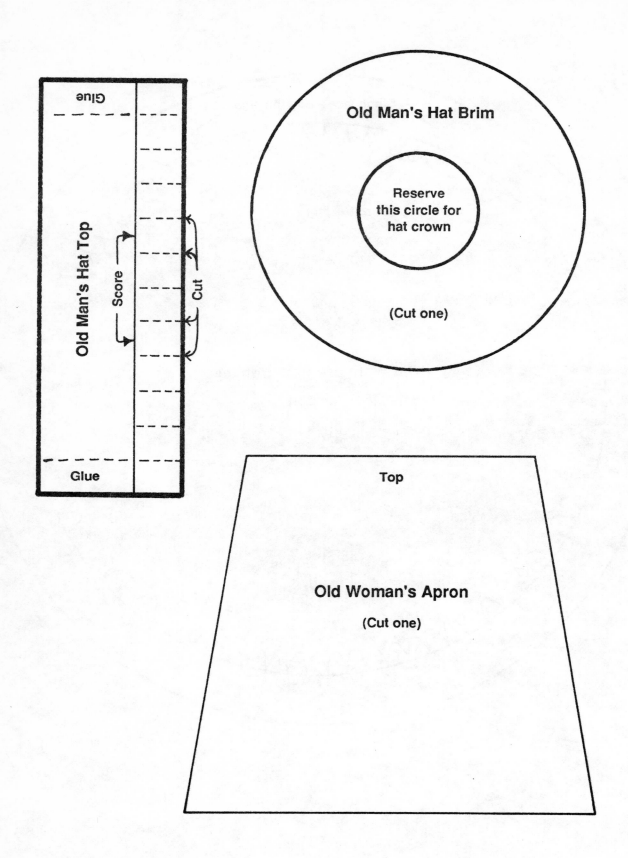

Old Man's Hat Top

Glue

Glue

Score

Cut

Old Man's Hat Brim

Reserve
this circle for
hat crown

(Cut one)

Top

Old Woman's Apron

(Cut one)

THE HOCA'S THREE SERMONS

Several hundred years ago in Turkey there lived in the town of Ak Shehir a man called Nasreddin Hoca. *(PRONOUNCED NAHZ-RE-DIN HOE-DJAH. BRING PUPPET OUT TOP OF BOX TO BE INTRODUCED TO THE AUDIENCE)* Nasreddin added the honorary title Hoca to his name when he became the teacher-priest. In fact he served as religious teacher, as Moslem priest, and sometimes as judge in local disputes. The Hoca had the peculiar habit of behaving very wisely in foolish situations and very foolishly when he was trying to be wise. Tales about him, some historical and some legendary, are still told and loved today.

Nasreddin Hoca was generally a happy man who enjoyed life. He liked to ride his beloved little donkey to a nearby town, visit with his friends in the coffee house, work in the vineyards, or just sit in the sun in his own courtyard. Six days each week he was free to do any of these activities. He had no schedules to keep and was free to follow his own inclinations.

But Friday! Friday was different because that was the day that all good Moslems went to their mosques. And because the Hoca was the priest, each Friday he was expected to climb the many stairs to the

127

pulpit of the mosque and deliver a sermon. It was fine for the Hoca to preach his sermon when he had something to say. But sometimes on Friday he could think of nothing important enough to talk about.

One Friday Nasreddin Hoca walked very slowly through the cobblestoned streets to the mosque. He walked slowly because he had no sermon prepared. He watched as the veiled women slipped up to the balcony of the mosque and as the men squatted on their soft thick rugs. No thoughts came to him. *(SLOWLY MOVE PUPPET UP THE BOX STAIRCASE)* He climbed the long staircase slowly, all the while studying the beauty of the mosque in hopes of receiving an inspiration. But no sermon manifested itself. At last he stood in his high pulpit and knew that he must say something.

"Oh, good people of Ak Shehir!" he called to the people congregated in the mosque. "Do you know what I am about to say to you?"

"No!" shouted the men, squatting on their rugs, and "no," whispered the women in the balcony.

"You do not know?" asked the Hoca. "Then it would surely be useless to talk to people who know nothing about this important subject. My words would be wasted."

And with that the Hoca walked slowly down the steps, *(MOVE*

128

PUPPET DOWN THE STAIRCASE AND INTO THE BOX) out of the mosque and was free.

"No more sermons until next Friday!" sighed the relieved Hoca to himself.

But even the cheerful Hoca could not help feeling a bit uncomfortable as the week progressed, for no thoughts were coming to mind for his next sermon. All too quickly Friday came and the Hoca had nothing to say to the people.

Even slower than last week he walked through the cobblestoned streets to the mosque. With sinking heart he watched the veiled women slip up to the balcony and the men squat on their rugs. One step at a time he mounted the stairs to the pulpit. *(CLIMB STAIRS)* At last he looked out over the upturned faces.

"Oh, people of Ak Shehir!" called out the Hoca. "Do you know what I am about to say to you?"

Remembering last Friday, the men replied, "Yes," and the women echoed, "yes."

"You know what I am about to say?" said the Hoca looking first at one side of the group and then at the other. "Since you know what I am about to say, there is no need for me to say it. It would be a useless waste of my time and yours to tell you something that you already know."

So saying, Nasreddin Hoca turned and *(DESCEND STAIRS)* slowly descended the stairs leading from the pulpit to the sunny out-of-doors. He was free for yet another week.

The week passed more quickly than Nasreddin Hoca would have wished, for he still had not a single thought for his sermon. When Friday came, he trudged slower than ever before along the cobblestoned streets to the mosque. *(CLIMB STAIRS)* With dismay he watched the veiled women find their places in the balcony and the men squat on their rugs. All his people were waiting, expecting him to say something solemn and worthy, but his mind was as empty as a cloudless sky. Still, his people were waiting; he had to say something.

"Oh, people of Ak Shehir!" intoned the Hoca searching his mind helplessly for an idea. "Do you know what I am about to say to you?"

"No," answered half the people, remembering last Friday.

"Yes," answered the other half of the people, remembering the Friday before last.

"So, some of you know what I am about to say and some of you do not." The Hoca rubbed his hands together and his eyes began to

130

twinkle. "That is very fine," he said. "Those of you who know may now tell those of you who do not know."

And with that Nasreddin Hoca skipped lightly down the stairs *(DESCEND STAIRS)* from the pulpit and out into the sunshine. He was free again -- free, at least, until the next Friday rolled around.

> *--Adapted from the Turkish tale*
> *for a lap puppet play*

This adaptation of a traditional Turkish tale is designed to be told using a box stage and hand puppet. The storyteller should tell the story in best oral tradition. On his or her lap should be a cardboard box about 12 to 15 inches square with the top and the bottom removed. A cardboard staircase leading to a pulpit should extend out the top of the box. Inside the box the storyteller holds the Hoca puppet who emerges only to climb the stairs to the pulpit. The puppet then addresses his sermon to the live audience thus allowing the children to become active participants in the story.

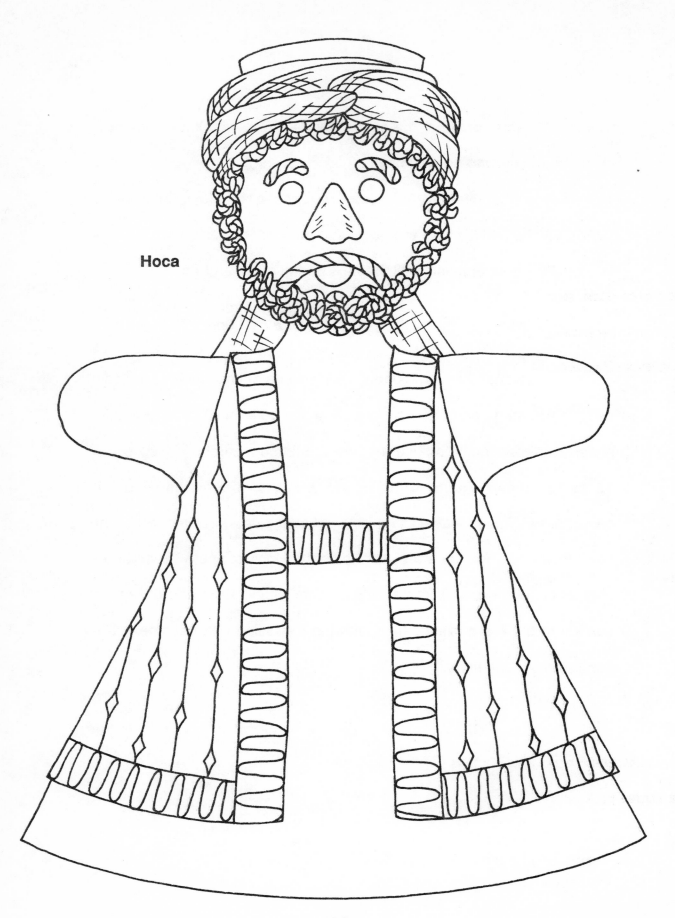

Hoca

To make the hoca puppet, use the following directions.

1. For the head use a 2 1/2" styrofoam ball; carve a hole about 1 1/2" deep to form the "neck" for attaching the cloth body.

2. Glue on black yarn for hair, beard, moustache and eyebrows. It is not necessary to cover entire head with hair, only the area surrounding face. To make curly hair, wrap yarn around a pencil to the length of one curl, about 2". Use a needle and thread; run needle through each strand on two or three sides of the pencil. Knot to fasten tightly. Remove curl and glue to side of head. Repeat until you have enough curls to make a full head of hair.

3. Use felt for facial features: eyes of dark brown, nose of tan, and mouth of red. For nose, glue side edges and top point only, bending piece vertically along center, slightly forward for a three dimensional effect.

4. For the turban, glue a shaving cream cap to crown of head. Measure 2 yards of 3" stretch bandaging gauze. Measure 7" from one end of

gauze. Hold with finger at bottom center front of cap. Twist remaining gauze loosely, while wrapping around cap loosely, leaving approximately 1/4" to 3/8" of cap uncovered at top edge. Wrap until desired fullness is achieved. Loop the two ends together, as shown, at center front base of wrapping.

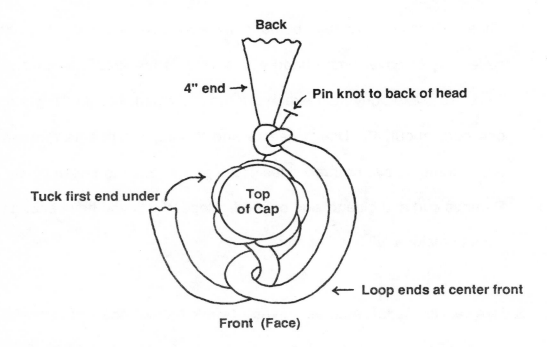

Tuck first end under wrappings at back. Secure with pin, hiding head of pin and making sure pin point does not protrude finger hole. Tie a loose knot in remaining end. Position knot at back center base of turban. Secure with pin as above. Trim off remaining gauze leaving a 4" end to hang down puppet's back.

5. For the hoca's body use felt, velvet or a soft luxurious fabric to simulate priests' robes.   For the vest, use felt or a rich-patterned brocade or upholstery material, preferably a fabric that will have a clean raw edge and finishing is unnecessary. If turning under raw edge is necessary, use armhole hem allowance on vest pattern.

Trace the top and bottom pieces of the puppet's basic body pattern. Overlap the top and bottom pieces where indicated to form the continuous body pattern.

Pin the pattern to the fabric and cut along outer solid line. Cut 6 1/2" length of braid for belt. Position on right side of body front piece at waistline. Stitch. Place right sides of front and back pieces together. Sew around sides and top allowing 3/8" seam allowance. Clip all curved seams close to the stitching line. Turn right side out and press seams flat. Hem or zigzag bottom if not felt.

6. For the vest cut out the back and two fronts. With right sides together, sew shoulder and side seams. If using armhole hem allowance, turn under and sew. Sew braid along bottom edge of vest, turning under

raw ends of braid to wrong side of vest fronts. Sew braid along fronts and back edge in one continuous piece turning under raw ends of braid to wrong side of vest front bottoms.

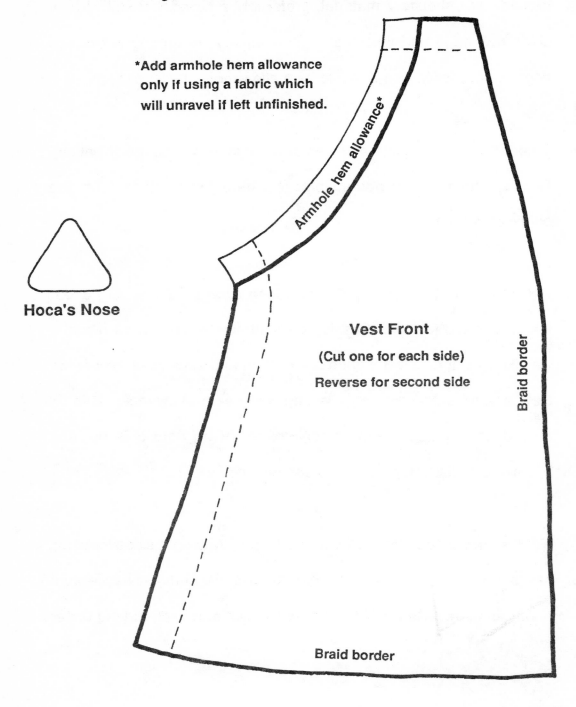

*Add armhole hem allowance only if using a fabric which will unravel if left unfinished.

Armhole hem allowance*

Hoca's Nose

Vest Front

(Cut one for each side)

Reverse for second side

Braid border

Braid border

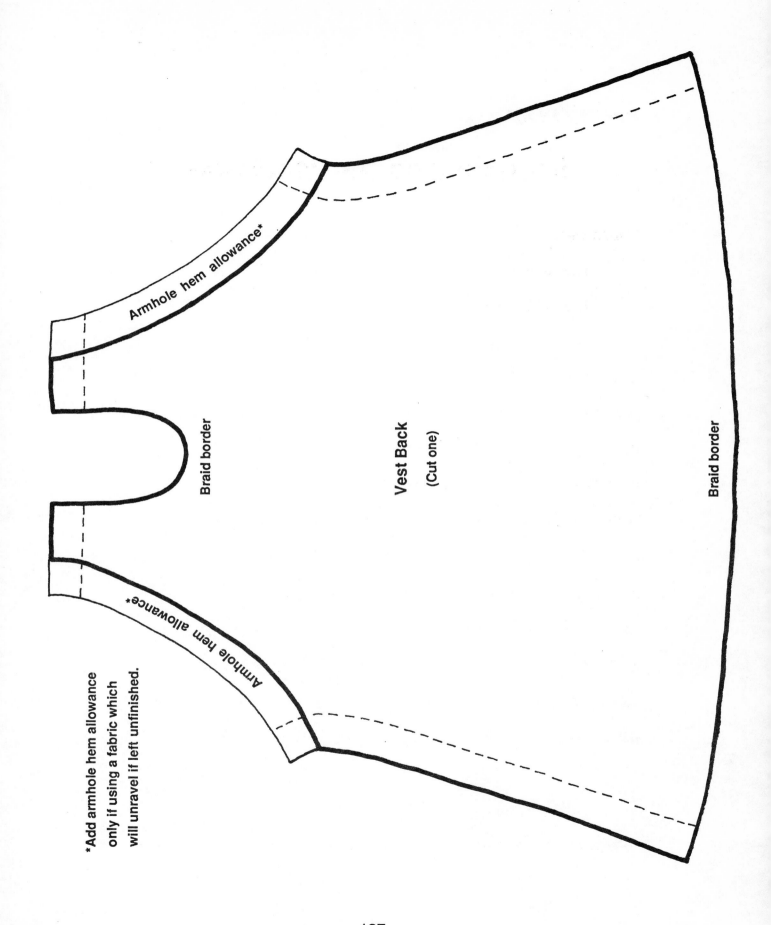

Armhole hem allowance*

Braid border

Vest Back

(Cut one)

Braid border

Braid border

Armhole hem allowance*

*Add armhole hem allowance only if using a fabric which will unravel if left unfinished.

137

PUPPET PLAY

THE HARE AND THE HEDGEHOG

Characters:

    Hedgehog

    Mrs. Hedgehog

    Hare

SCENE I

(AT RISE: HEDGEHOG IS WALKING THROUGH THE VEGETABLE GARDEN)

HEDGEHOG: Such a fine Sunday morning! The cowslips are lovely in the meadow and the sun is shining warmly. Such a fine lazy day! *(WHISTLES A TUNE)* My, these turnips are doing well; it is a good thing that I decided to come to the garden and check on them while Mrs. Hedgehog is washing the children. *(INSPECTS TURNIPS. SEES HARE AND BOWS)* Good Morning.

HARE: And how does it happen that you are out so early this morning?

HEDGEHOG: I am taking a walk and inspecting my turnips.

HARE: A walk! Surely you can find something better to do with those crooked legs of yours.

HEDGEHOG: *(ANGRILY)* Do you mean to say, sir, that you think that

138

your legs are better than mine?

HARE: Yes, I would say so.

HEDGEHOG: And I say they are not. In fact, start fair in a race and I shall beat you. Yes, I can beat you every time.

HARE: A race, my dear friend Hedgehog? You? You must not be feeling well! But on the other hand, what would you like to bet?

HEDGEHOG: I'll wager a gold coin.

HARE: Agreed. Shake hands on it and let the race begin.

HEDGEHOG: What's the hurry? I haven't even had breakfast yet. Let's meet back here in half an hour for the race.

HARE: Very well. *(HARE EXITS RIGHT, HEDGEHOG EXITS LEFT)*

SCENE II

(HEDGEHOG AND MRS. HEDGEHOG ENTER LEFT)

MRS. HEDGEHOG: I still don't understand why you are dragging me down to the turnip patch at this time of day. And right when I was washing the children, besides.

HEDGEHOG: If you will just listen, I am trying to explain. I need you to be at the turnip patch now.

MRS. HEDGEHOG: But why now?

HEDGEHOG: *(CASUALLY)* Oh, nothing, really. It's just that I bet Hare a gold coin that I could beat him in a race, and I want you to be there to see it.

MRS. HEDGEHOG: Are you out of your mind? You can never win a race with a hare.

HEDGEHOG: No more scolding, please, Wife. I beg you, just do as I say.

MRS. HEDGEHOG: *(SIGHING)* Very well, what must I do?

HEDGEHOG: Do you see those furrows in the field? That is where the race will be run. The Hare will run in one furrow and I will run in another. You, my dear, must go to the far end of the field and lie down in *my* furrow. Do not make a sound. When you hear Hare coming close to the end of his furrow, jump up quickly and shout, "Here I am already!" Do you understand?

MRS. HEDGEHOG: Yes, I understand. When Hare approaches, I am to jump up and shout, "Here I am already."

HEDGEHOG: Very good. *(MRS. HEDGEHOG GOES TO THE END OF FURROW AND LIES DOWN--LOWER PUPPET OUT OF SIGHT. ENTER HARE)* Oh, there you are, Hare. I was beginning to wonder if you had changed your mind about the race.

HARE: Not at all. When do we start?

HEDGEHOG: Right now. Let's see...you run in that furrow and I'll run in this one. Agreed?

HARE: Agreed! *(HEDGEHOG AND HARE TAKE PLACES)* On your mark, get set, GO! *(HARE RUNS FAST, HEDGEHOG TAKES A FEW STEPS AND DUCKS DOWN IN FURROW)*

HARE: Wow! I'll show Hedgehog a thing or two about running. Already I'm about there.

MRS. HEDGEHOG: *(JUMPING UP)* Here I am already!

HARE: No! How could you have beat me? Impossible! I cannot believe it! I demand another race. Back to the end of the furrow. On your mark, get set, go! *(HARE RUNS, MRS. HEDGEHOG DROPS DOWN INTO FURROW)* I'm running so fast that my ears will hardly stay on my head. This time Hedgehog cannot possible beat me. *(AS HARE APPROACHES END OF FURROW, HEDGEHOG POPS UP)*

HEDGEHOG: Here I am already!

HARE: No, no! Not again! How could you beat me twice! One more race! Three for luck!

HEDGEHOG: Very well, Hare. I'll race as many times as you like.

HARE: Get set, go! *(HARE RUNS, HEDGEHOG DROPS DOWN INTO*

141

FURROW) This time I'm nearly flying. I've never run so fast. I am sure to win this race.

MRS. HEDGEHOG: *(JUMPING UP)* Here I am already!

HARE: It cannot be! Impossible! Back to the end of the furrow! I--cannot--lose--this time. Puff, puff! I must--beat--that hedgehog.

HEDGEHOG: Here I am already!

HARE: Enough! I give up! My legs are so tired I can run no more. The gold coins are yours. *(EXITS, GASPING)*

HEDGEHOG: *(PICKING UP GOLD COINS)* Wife! Oh, come, Wife. The race is over now and as you can see, I have won. I hope that you are sorry that you doubted my ability to run. For now you have seen for yourself that I beat that Hare in four races. And I'm not even tired! Come, let's go home now and fetch the children. *(BOTH EXIT)*

--Adapted from the English tale
for puppets

The background set, either of black scrim, cardboard, or foam core board, should be painted to look like a vegetable garden with long horizontal furrows. The stick puppets, made from the accompanying patterns, can easily appear and disappear in the furrows.

To make the puppets, use stiff posterboard. Cut one hare pattern as shown and cut one pattern reversed so features and outline are facing opposite direction. Cut two hedgehog patterns as shown and cut two hedgehog patterns with features reversed. Color figures and outline features with bold lines. Glue one stick each to backs of one hare and two hedgehog figures. Match remaining figures to these and glue wrong sides together resulting in three two-sided stick puppets: one hare and two hedgehogs. These puppets can now turn around and change directions as needed in the story.

Hare

Hedgehog

PUPPET PLAY

THE BEAR SAYS "NORTH"

Characters: **Properties:**

    Osmo the Bear   Quail

    Mikko the Fox   Bush

At rise Osmo the Bear is slightly right of center stage. He speaks slowly and methodically. Hidden behind a bush is the quail. Attach a thread to the quail; allow the thread to drape loosely across the stage and be held by puppeteer off stage left.

OSMO: Everyone is always teasing me about being so clumsy and slow. Every day they tease, tease, tease. If only I could show them how fine I really am. But wait! There in those bushes I see a huge, fat quail. If only I could catch that quail...then everyone would say how great I am, and no one would dare to tease me again. If only I can catch it...I would show them all, especially that smart old fox Mikko. *(BEGINS TO STALK QUAIL)* Careful now...careful... *(POUNCES AND CATCHES QUAIL IN HIS MOUTH. ENTER MIKKO FROM STAGE LEFT. OSMO PARADES PROUDLY UP AND DOWN IN FRONT OF HIM HOLDING THE QUAIL IN HIS MOUTH)*

MIKKO: Well, hello, Osmo.

OSMO: *(NODS HEAD)*

MIKKO: *(ASIDE TO AUDIENCE)* Aha! That clumsy, pokey Osmo has somehow caught a quail and is trying to boast of it. I shall completely ignore his fine catch and see what happens.

(OSMO CONTINUES TO PARADE EXPECTANTLY UP AND DOWN IN FRONT OF MIKKO)

MIKKO: I say, Osmo, which way is the wind blowing today? *(STICKS HIS NOSE IN THE AIR AND SNIFFS)*

OSMO: *(SHAKES HIS HEAD)* Um! Um! Um!

MIKKO: Really, Osmo, what did you say? Which way is the wind blowing?

OSMO: *(SHAKES HIS HEAD MORE VIGOROUSLY)* UM! UM! UM!

MIKKO: You say, dear Osmo, that the wind is blowing from the South? Are you sure?

OSMO: *(SHAKES HIS HEAD DESPERATELY, ANGRILY)* Um! Um! Um!

MIKKO: Indeed, Osmo, what did you say? It's not from the South? Then which direction is it blowing?

OSMO: *(FURIOUSLY AND LOUDLY)* "North!" *(WHEN HE OPENS HIS MOUTH TO TALK, THE QUAIL FLIES AWAY. PULL QUAIL*

THROUGH THE AIR AND OFF STAGE LEFT BY THE ATTACHED

STRING) Now just see what you have done!

MIKKO: I? I, Osmo? What have I done?

OSMO: You've made me lose my quail, that's what you have done.

MIKKO: (INNOCENTLY) Why, Osmo, how can you say such a thing? I

did nothing at all.

OSMO: You kept asking which way the wind is blowing. And when I

opened my mouth to answer, my fine, lovely quail flew away.

MIKKO: Why, Osmo, why ever did you open your mouth?

OSMO: How could I say "North" without opening my mouth?

MIKKO: (LAUGHING) Don't blame me, Osmo. If I had had the quail in

my mouth and you asked me which way the wind was blowing, I would

never have opened my mouth to say "North."

OSMO: What would you have done?

MIKKO: Very simple, my dear friend Osmo. I would have kept my teeth

tight together like this and said "East!"

(OSMO EXITS STAGE RIGHT ANGRILY, MIKKO EXITS STAGE LEFT

CHUCKLING)

> *--Adapted from the Norse*
> *tale for puppets*

The backdrop or scrim for this play should include some bushes and trees. Remember that a quail nests on the ground and does not perch in trees. The background scenery can be vague and abstract for it provides no essential information relating to the story.

The bear, fox, and quail patterns should be cut from stiff posterboard. Features can be colored with markers or paints or colored papers. Outline all features with bold lines. To make the bear and the fox, glue ears behind head where indicated. Glue mouth under fold of brown paper lunch bag bottom. Glue head to paper bag bottom lining up with mouth.

To make the quail, fold 12" x 14" white posterboard in half along 12" length. Place quail pattern on fold where indicated. Trace shape and transfer features. Cut along shape leaving fold line uncut. Fold shape to remaining side of posterboard. Trace around figure. Cut out second shape leaving both shapes linked at fold line. Color in features with markers, outlining in bold lines. Color both sides, if desired, reversing features for second side. (Suggested colors: brown face and wing with white stripes and breast and black neck ring, crown, and plume. Punch out breast holes on both sides of quail. Stick reinforcement label behind each hole so yarn or string will not tear hole when pulled off stage. Masking tape or other strong tape may be used instead; cut hole through tape. Score along bottom flap fold lines on backs of both quail shapes. Slit bottom flaps where shown. Insert both bottom flaps together at slits. Tie yarn or string through both breast holes making sure yarn is long enough for your stage.

To make the bush fold a 9" x 20" piece of posterboard (preferably two-sided green) in half along 9" length. Place bush pattern along fold line where indicated. Continue following instructions given for cutting out quail. Color bush with different shades of green. Outline details with bold lines. Assemble base as quail.

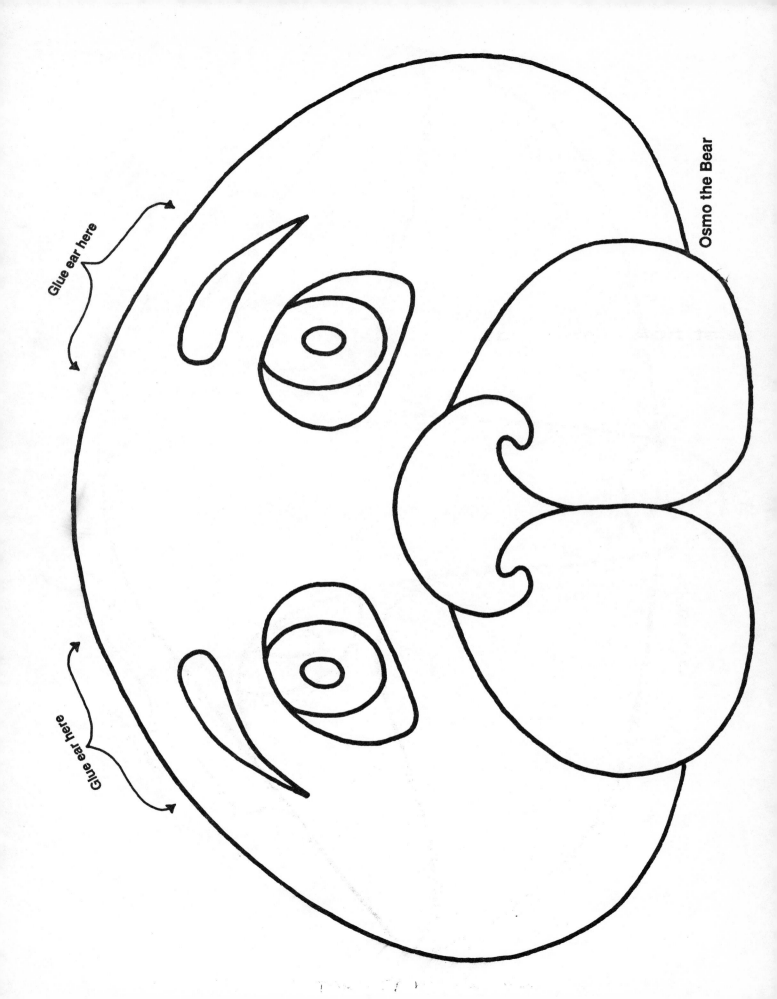

Glue ear here

Glue ear here

Osmo the Bear

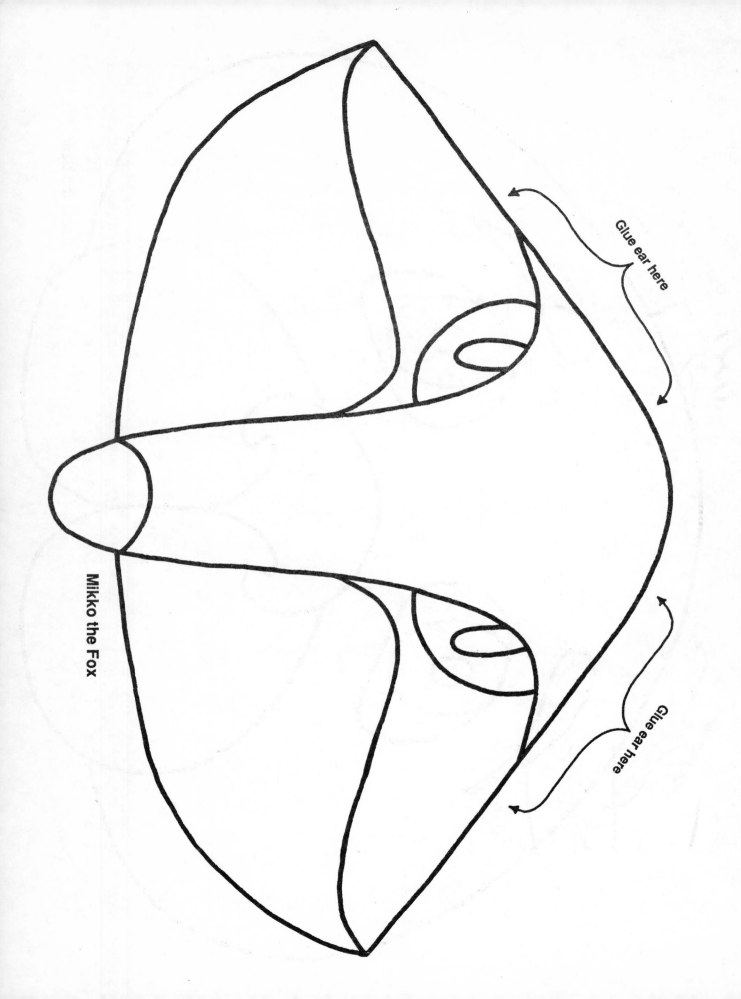

Mikko the Fox

Glue ear here

Glue ear here

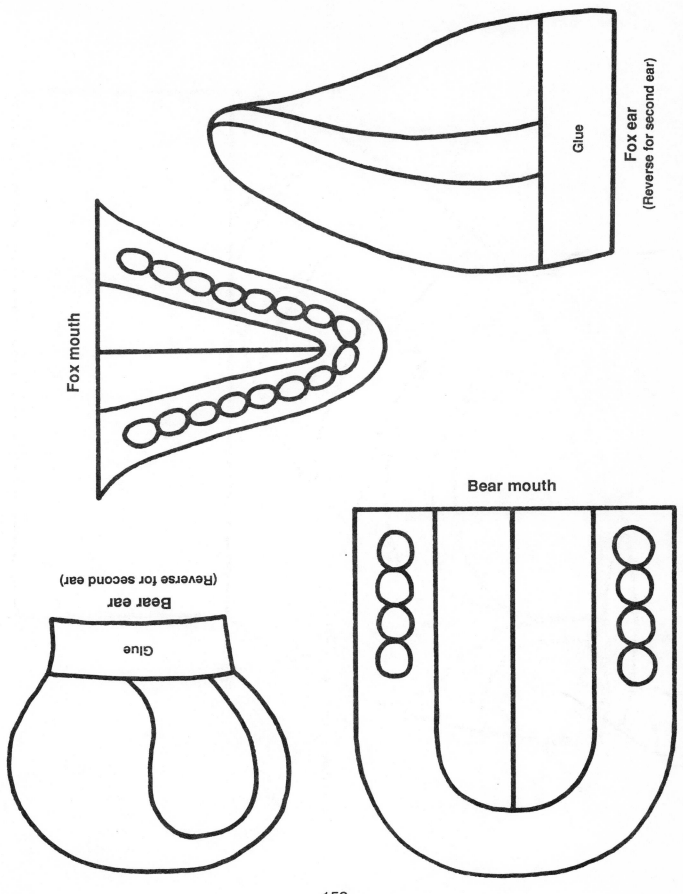

Fox ear
(Reverse for second ear)

Glue

Fox mouth

Bear mouth

Bear ear
(Reverse for second ear)

Glue

153

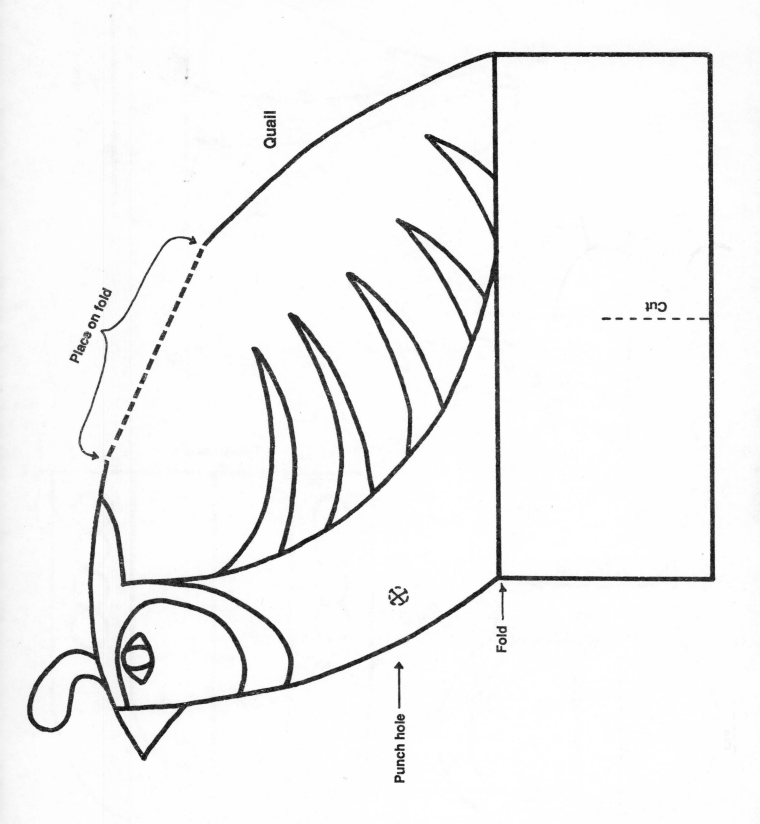

Quail

Place on fold

Cut

Fold

Punch hole

154

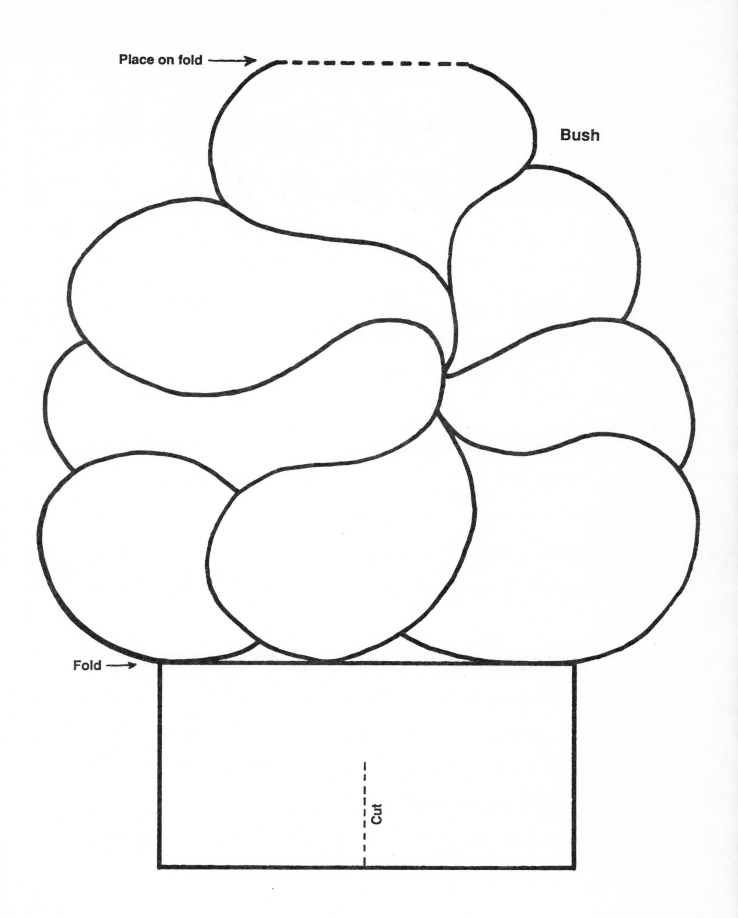

Place on fold →

Bush

Fold →

Cut

155

THE MILLER, THE BOY,
AND THE DONKEY

Characters:

Miller	Girl	Townsman
Boy	Old Man	
Donkey	Woman	

Open with musical introduction. Place miller and boy on the "road" just behind the donkey. Boy's hand can be placed on donkey's back. Turn on spotlight just as music diminishes and before the narrator begins. For each scene change, turn off spotlight, increase volume of music, make necessary changes, diminish music, and turn on spotlight.

Some time ago a miller and his son were taking their donkey to sell at a nearby marketplace. All three walked along cheerfully until they saw a young girl coming toward them. *(PLACE GIRL ON STAGE FACING GROUP)* As she approached, she giggled, shaking her head from side to side with mirth.

"What fools you are," she exclaimed, "to walk in the hot sun when you could be riding your donkey." And still laughing, she walked past them down the road.

(REMOVE GIRL. PLACE BOY ASTRIDE DONKEY'S BACK. MILLER WALKS BEHIND DONKEY)

The miller frowned slightly and bade the boy mount the donkey. He himself walked before the beast as they continued toward the market.

(PLACE OLD MAN BESIDE ROAD FACING GROUP)

Soon they encountered an old man standing beside the road, muttering to himself. "Just look at that," he was saying, "youth today have no respect for their elders. There that lazy lad rides the donkey while the old man walks. Tsk! Tsk!"

(REMOVE OLD MAN)

Now the miller happened to overhear the old man, and he certainly did not want his son to appear ill-mannered. At once he told the boy to get down and walk behind the donkey while he himself rode.

(PLACE BOY ON ROAD BEHIND DONKEY. PLACE MILLER ASTRIDE DONKEY)

As the sun rose in the sky, the miller's son began to feel hot and tired and began to lag further and further behind. *(PLACE BOY FURTHER BEHIND DONKEY. PLACE WOMAN ON ROAD FACING MILLER)* A woman returning from the marketplace took in the situation in a glance and began to rail at the miller.

"How dare you ride the donkey when your poor child can barely limp along! You should be ashamed of yourself."

(REMOVE WOMAN. PLACE BOY ON DONKEY BEHIND MILLER)

The miller nodded to the woman in embarrassment and pulled his son up behind him.

(PLACE MAN ON ROAD FACING GROUP)

As they neared their destination, one of the townsmen called out, "Is that your donkey, friend? One would hardly think so from the way in which you over-burden it. Why, you could sooner carry the little fellow yourself than he can carry the two of you."

(REMOVE MAN. PLACE MILLER AND BOY ON GROUND. PLACE DONKEY ON THEIR SHOULDERS)

With a sigh the miller dismounted and helped his son down. "Very well, son," he said, "let us carry the donkey." And with much effort they lifted the animal and started down the road.

(PLACE BRIDGE ON CENTER STAGE. REMOVE DONKEY. PLACE MILLER AND BOY ON BRIDGE WITH ARMS OUTSTRETCHED)

As they drew closer to the town, they crossed a bridge over a river.

The struggling creature pulled from their grasp and jumped over the bridge. The miller and the boy rushed to rescue their donkey.

(REMOVE BRIDGE. PLACE BOY ON ROAD LEADING DONKEY. PLACE MILLER BEHIND DONKEY)

"My son," the miller stated firmly, "we have tried to please everyone and in fact have pleased no one. From now on we will try only to please ourselves."

(PLACE MILLER SLIGHTLY AHEAD OF BOY AND DONKEY)

And with that he and the boy led the donkey down the road to the marketplace.

(BRING UP MUSIC AFTER NARRATOR'S LAST LINE. TURN OFF SPOTLIGHT AND PLAY MUSIC TO END--ABOUT 30 SECONDS)

*--Adapted from Aesop's **Fables**
for puppets*

This play is designed for shadow puppets. A shadow puppet theater can be made by stretching a white sheet tightly across a doorway, between two poles, over a large frame made from a cardboard box, or across the opening of a standard puppet theater. The shadow puppets can be traced from the accompanying patterns; they are then pressed against the sheet. When a strong light is placed BEHIND the stage, it causes the puppets to cast silhouettes on the other side of the screen where the audience is seated.

To make the puppets, trace each of the following figures on light-weight, stiff cardboard. Cut out. Match the pieces of each puppet and attach by inserting a paper fastener at each X. Punch holes at the O's. Push a pipe cleaner through one hole (from the back of the puppet) and back through the other. Insert the pipe cleaner in a plastic soda straw and push the straw up to the hole in the puppet. This provides a sturdy rod for manipulating the puppet.

The Miller, The Boy, and The Donkey can be presented as a pantomime (characters moving) or as a tableau (characters stationary). The instructions included in the script are for the tableau.

Scenery in the form of a border around the opening of the theater can contribute a great deal to the mood. Poster board cut to resemble grass, shrubs, and trees on all four sides of the stage can be very effective.

Carefully selected music provides a satisfying introduction as well as a bridge between scenes. At each indicated location in the script, turn off the spotlight, bring up the music slightly, make all necessary scene changes, turn down the music, and turn on the spotlight.

Perhaps the simplest way to present the play is by recording all narration and music in advance. Practicing with the tape will help in achieving a polished performance.

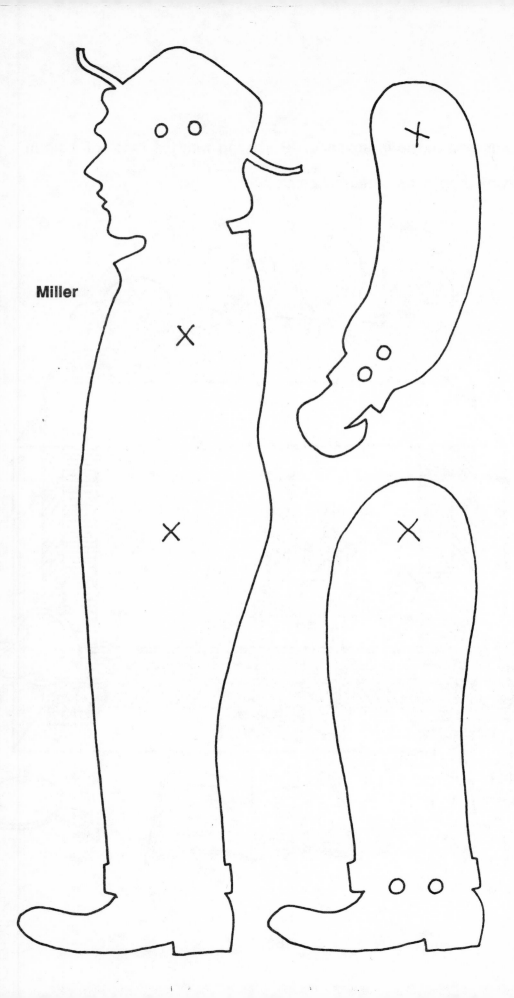

Miller

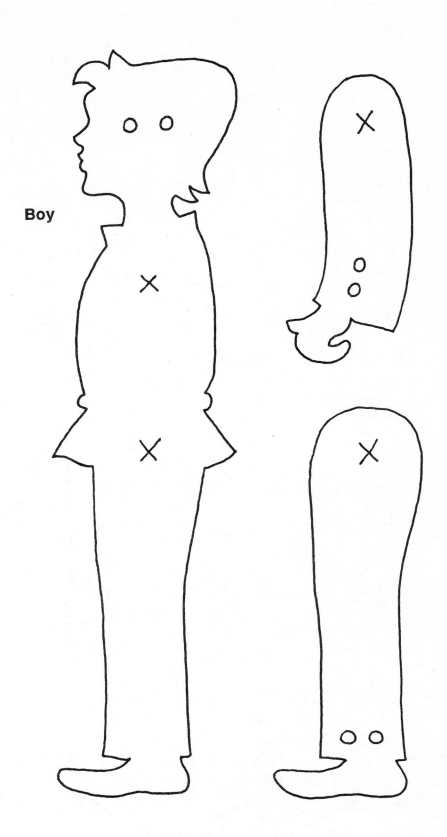

Boy

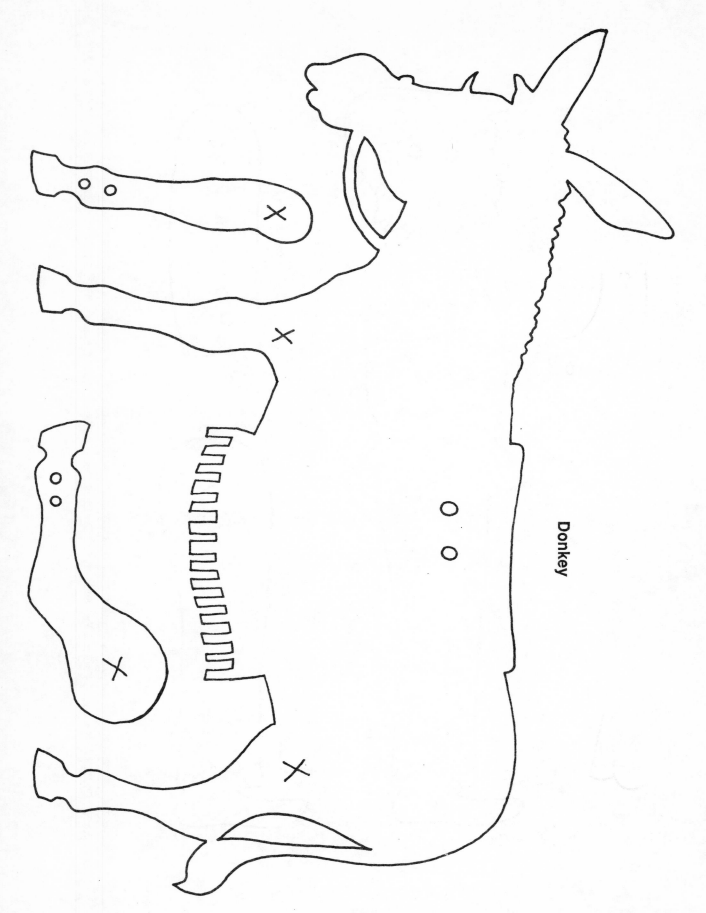

Donkey

164

Girl

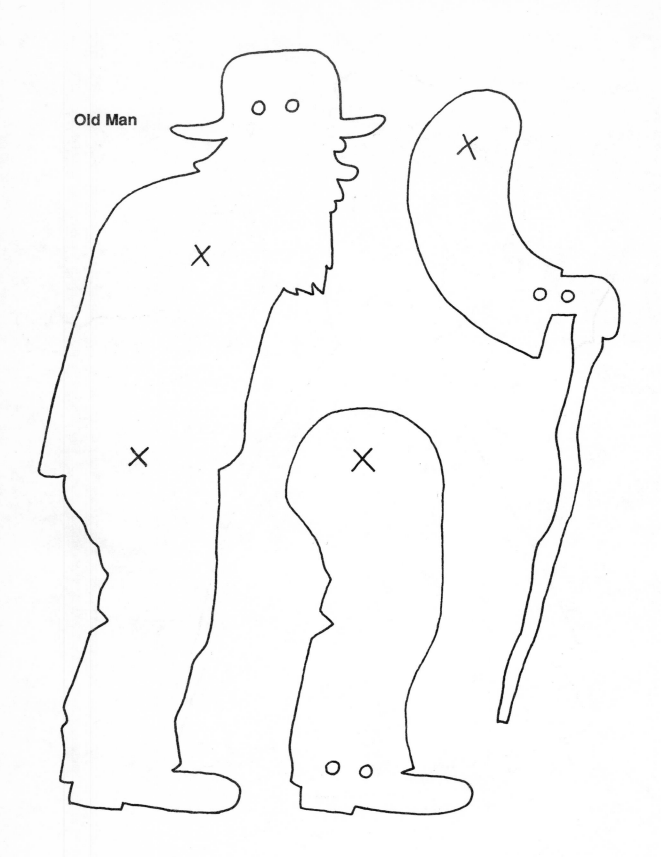

Old Man

Woman

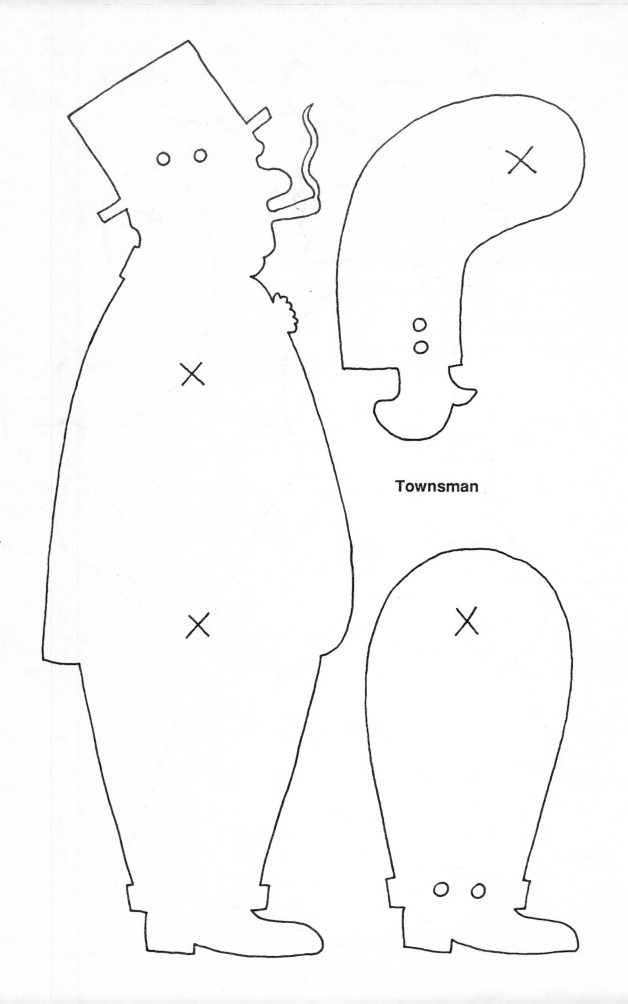

Townsman

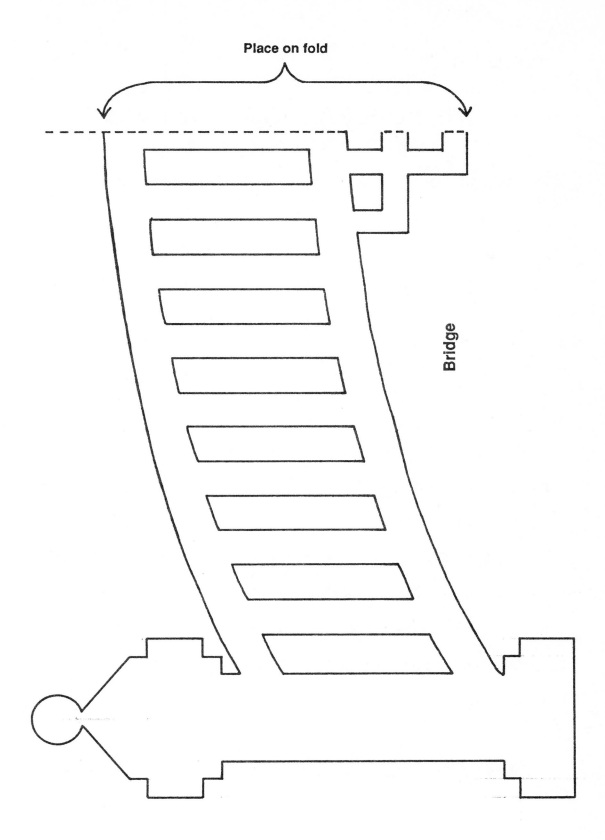

Place on fold

Bridge

169

THE SORCERER'S APPRENTICE

Characters: **Properties:**

    Narrator   Water jar

    Sorcerer   Broom

    Fritz, the apprentice   Broom with buckets

                                                       Two brooms with buckets

                                                       Book of spells

Setting

The sorcerer's home. A chair and a table are in the room (preferably painted on the backdrop), a broom stands in the corner, a huge cauldron (water jar) is conspicuous. The background set should be painted to enhance the idea of the sorcerer's home. A plain black scrim could be used if the puppet theater has stage lights. A long piece of foam core or heavy poster board about 18 inches wide should be painted to depict swirling water, with the top edge cut to correspond to wave crests.

NARRATOR: Once upon a time there was a sorcerer *(ENTER*

SORCERER) who was renowned for his remarkable skills in making magic. It was rumored that he knew at least ten thousand magic spells. His fame spread far and wide, and aspiring young magicians pleaded to study with him. From among these students the sorcerer selected as his apprentice *(ENTER FRITZ)* a boy named Fritz.

SORCERER: Young man, your job here is to sweep the floor and keep the house clean and tidy. Above all, you must keep this jar filled with water from the river.

FRITZ: Yes, sir. But I want to learn to do magic.

SORCERER: Do these jobs well and in time you will learn magic.

NARRATOR: The sorcerer's apprentice did the jobs well, day in and day out. And true to his word the sorcerer occasionally rewarded him by teaching him a simple spell. As time passed Fritz grew tired of his assignments and, sad to say, even became a bit lazy. He often allowed the water jar to remain less than full. One day the sorcerer was called to a nearby town to perform magic.

SORCERER: Fritz, I shall be gone the entire day. When I return, I expect to find the water jar brimful and the house tidy.

FRITZ: Yes, sir. You can be sure that I will do just as you say.

(EXIT SORCERER THROUGH DOOR STAGE LEFT)

NARRATOR: But the sorcerer was barely out of sight when his apprentice began to complain.

FRITZ: *(PICKING UP THE BROOM AND HALF-HEARTEDLY SWEEPING)* All I do all day long day after day is work, work, work while the sorcerer has all the fun. I came here as his apprentice to learn magic, not to sweep and carry water. *(STANDS BROOM IN CORNER, SITS IN CHAIR)* Well, today I'm not sweeping any more! But what will I do about that water jar? I surely don't wish to waste my entire day carrying water from the river.

NARRATOR: As Fritz sat frowning at the water jar, he suddenly had an idea.

FRITZ: *(JUMPING FROM CHAIR)* Just yesterday the master said a spell that caused the broom to walk. If it can walk, it can work. If I can only remember the spell...let's see...Abracadabra...no, that's not it. Hocus pocus...no, that's not it either.

NARRATOR: Fritz continued to puzzle over the spell. Then with a knowing smile, he picked up a wand from the sorcerer's table and waved it toward the broom.

FRITZ: *(IN A LOUD, COMMANDING VOICE)* Broom, up! Fetch water from the river and fill the jar, please.

NARRATOR: The sorcerer's apprentice was shocked, but pleased to see the broom obey. The broom leaned out from the wall, shuddered and shook, picked up the bucket and swished out the door. *(EXIT STAGE LEFT)* A moment or two later it was back and emptied the full bucket into the water jar. Out the door it went, soon to return with yet another bucketful of water.

FRITZ: Ah, now that is more like it! *(WATCHES THE BROOM FOR A MINUTE, THEN SITS IN CHAIR WITH A LARGE BOOK)* Now while the broom fills the water jar, I will study the socerer's book of incantations. *(SETTLES DOWN WITH BOOK)*

NARRATOR: Fritz became so absorbed in his reading that he forgot to glance occasionally at the broom. He failed to notice that the water jar was full, and the broom failed to notice it also. It continued to pour water into the jar. The splashing of the overflowing water startled Fritz.

FRITZ: *(JUMPING UP)* Stop, broom, that's enough water! *(CHASES AFTER BROOM)* Stop! Stop, I say!

NARRATOR: But the busy broom ran past him for another bucket of water.

FRITZ: I made the broom work by using magic; surely I can make it stop by magic. Let me see, abracadabra...no, that didn't work. Hocus pocus...no, that didn't work, either. *(CLIMBS ONTO A CHAIR AND SAYS IN A LOUD AND CLEAR VOICE)* Broom, stop! Do not fetch any more water.

NARRATOR: But to the alarm of the apprentice, the broom did not seem to hear. It just poured another bucketful of water into the overflowing jar and started for the door. Fritz gave up on using magic. He looked around desperately and saw an ax near the door. He grabbed the ax and with a mighty blow chopped the broom into two pieces. *(DURING THIS SPEECH THE PUPPETEERS SHOULD EACH GRASP A BOTTOM OF THE PAINTED WATER AND LIFT IT UNTIL JUST THE PEAKS OF WATER ARE VISIBLE TO THE AUDIENCE. THEY SHOULD GRADUALLY RAISE THE WATER UNTIL THE SORCERER STOPS THE MAGIC)*

FRITZ: *(WIPING HIS BROW AND SIGHING)* At last I've stopped the broom. Now I must mop up this water before the sorcerer returns.

NARRATOR: But as Fritz stared in disbelief, the two pieces of the broom picked themselves up, shuddered and shook, and each picked up a bucket and headed for the river. With two brooms carrying water, the water filled the room twice as fast. Chairs and table began to float. The apprentice shouted at the brooms, but they merely hastened on with their chores.

FRITZ: Stop! Oh, brooms, please stop!

NARRATOR: The water swirled higher and higher and poor Fritz gave himself up for lost.

FRITZ: Help me! Help me! Please...please, help me! *(PUPPET SHOULD SUBMERGE AND REAPPEAR TWO OR THREE TIMES DURING THIS SPEECH)*

NARRATOR: Then above the terrible roar of the flooding water, the boy heard the voice of the sorcerer who had just that moment returned.

SORCERER: (HOLDING WAND HIGH) Stop! Go back to where you belong!

NARRATOR: Immediately, the water returned to the river and the broom in one piece again stood quietly in the corner. Fritz lay on the floor gasping for breath, not daring to look at his master. He shivered quietly, half expecting to be turned into a beetle or a worm. Slowly, he got to his feet.

FRITZ: I'm sorry, truly sorry. *(STANDS BEFORE THE SORCERER, HEAD BOWED)*

SORCERER: You have disobeyed me. You are unworthy of becoming a sorcerer. In fact you have received your last lesson in magic.

NARRATOR: And with that the sorcerer led the apprentice to the door and gave him such a terrific kick that he sailed right through it. So if you should ever desire to try a piece of magic on your own, remember that stopping a spell can be just as important as starting one.

--Adapted from the traditional
tale for the puppet stage

The sorcerer and the apprentice can be represented by either stick puppets or styrofoam ball hand puppets. To make the stick puppets, trace the patterns and transfer them onto posterboard. Color the sorcerer's hat and robe black with designs of silver and gold. Color the apprentice's hat and robe a bright color, possibly yellow or gold with red or blue trim. Tape a wooden ice cream stick to the back for a handle. To make the styrofoam ball puppets, use the following directions.

1. In a 2 1/2" styrofoam ball carve a hole about 1 1/2" deep to form the "neck" for attaching the cloth body.

2. Glue on heavy gray yarn strands for the sorcerer's hair and beard and brown yarn for the apprentice's hair. White glue diluted with water works well.

3. Glue on features of felt, sequins, or beads.

4. Make a cone of felt for each hat; glue or pin hats to styrofoam heads.

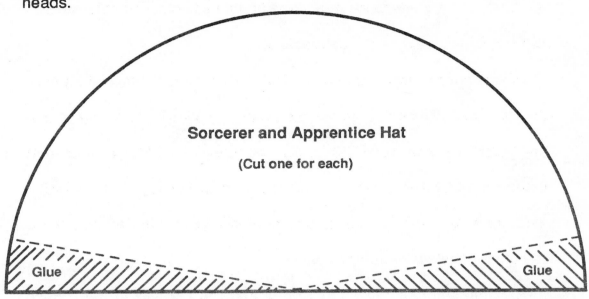

Sorcerer and Apprentice Hat

(Cut one for each)

Glue   Glue

5. Cut out two sides of each robe using the basic body pattern as a guide. Stitch the two sides together and turn so that the seams are inside.

6. Place your hand inside the body with your forefinger serving as the neck. Place the styrofoam ball head onto your forefinger and firmly adjust it so that it fits snugly and comfortably.

All other pieces (the brooms, the book, and the water jar) should be traced and transferred onto posterboard. Each should be appropriately colored with felt tip pens, crayons, or paints. Each should be taped to a thin wooden dowel stick or pencil. The water jar can then be attached to the back of the stage since it requires no movement. The other objects can be manipulated by the puppeteers.

Unless specific instructions are given for the action, simply dramatize the narration. Remember to move only the puppet who is talking so that the audience can readily identify the speaker. Movements and emotions must sometimes be exaggerated to convey the meanings. One puppeteer should manipulate the sorcerer and the brooms while the other handles the apprentice.

An important touch might include performing the play to a recording of *The Sorcerer's Apprentice* by Paul Dukas. With practice and planning the action can match the music.

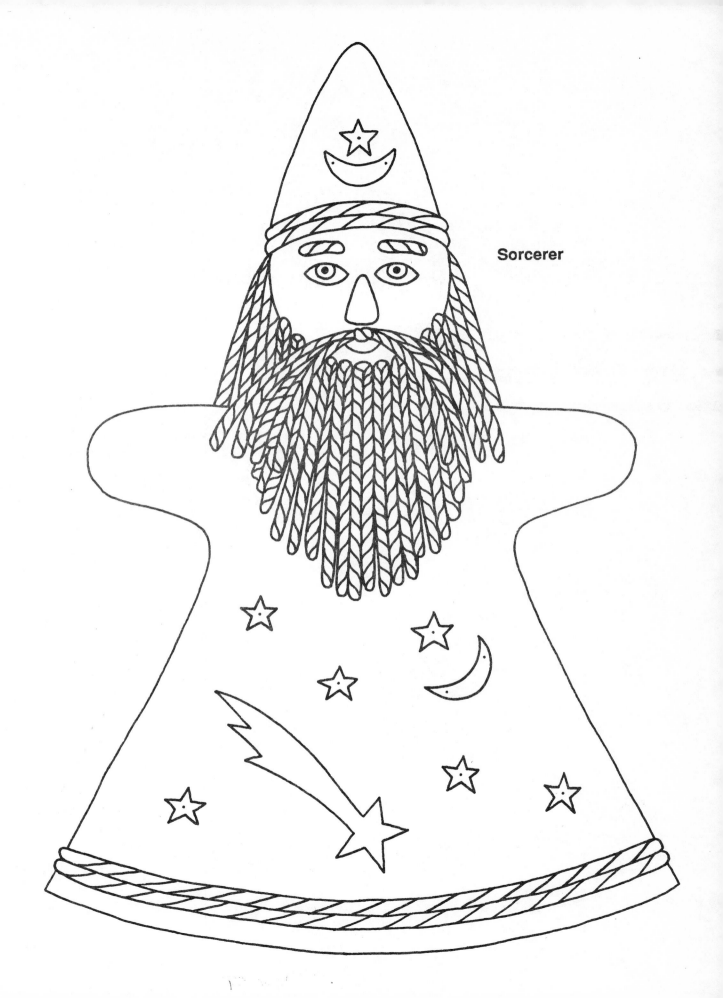

Sorcerer

Apprentice

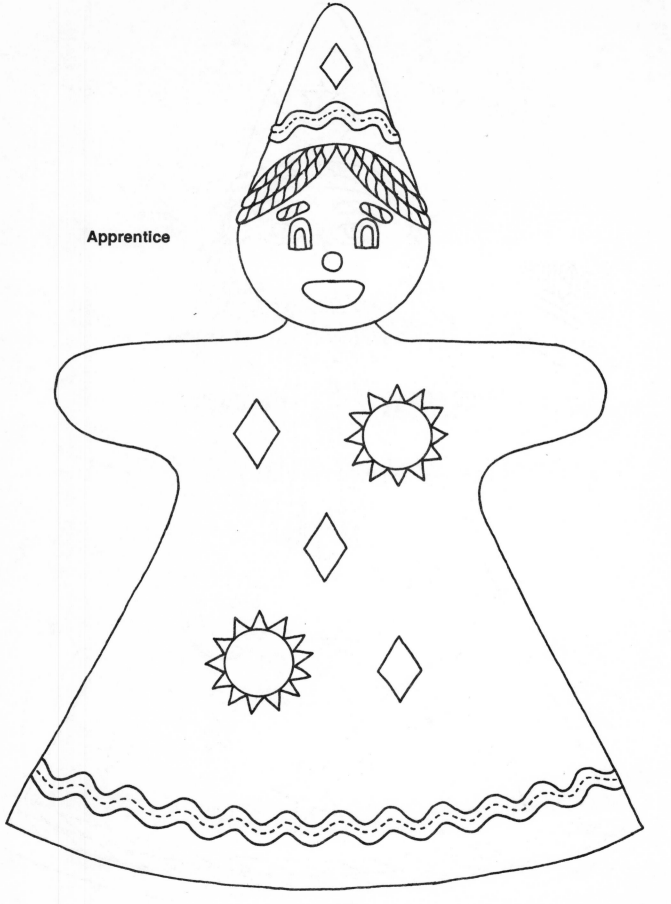

Book of Incantations

Star for Magic Wand

Water Jar

Broom

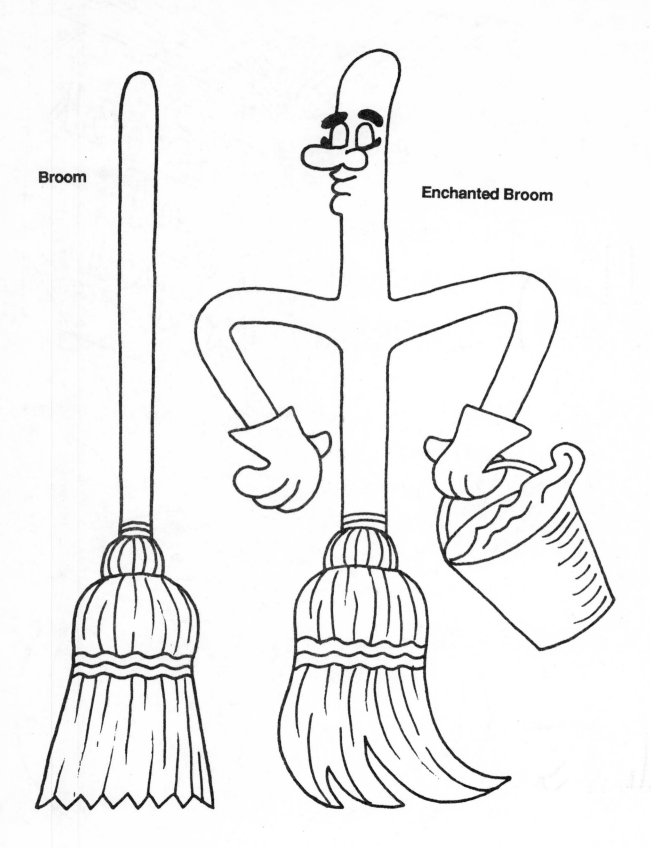

Enchanted Broom

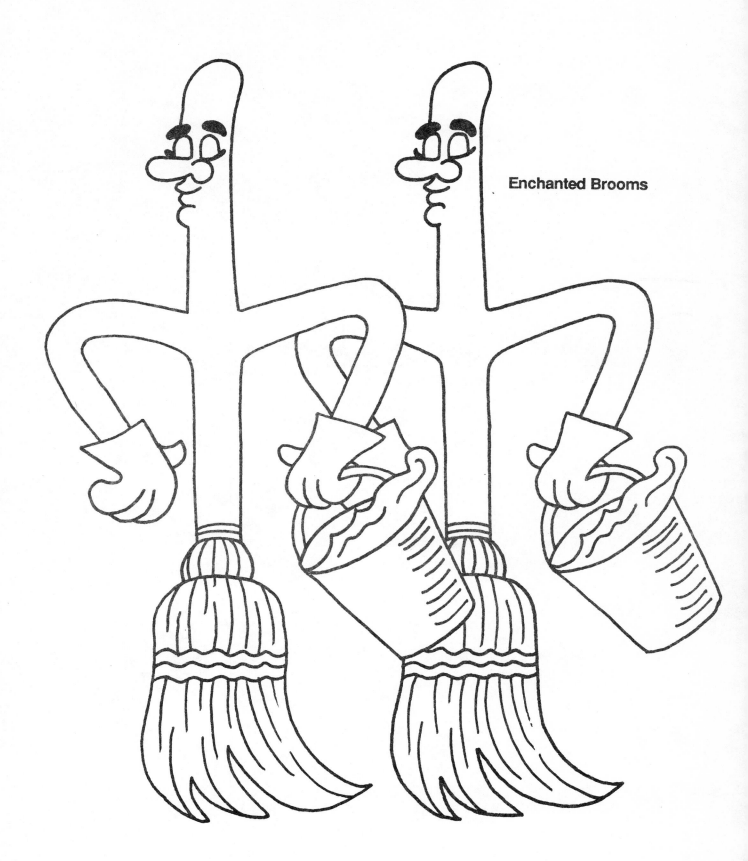

Enchanted Brooms

183

BIBLIOGRAPHY

This bibliography includes picture books, 16mm films, and 35mm sound filmstrips. All entries have been selected for their appropriateness for older children and for their usefulness in a group setting. Some of the picture books can be used with relatively large groups of boys and girls; others will work only with small groups. Films and filmstrips chosen for inclusion must accurately interpret children's literature and, hopefully, will stimulate viewers to seek out the original story, song, or verse.

BIBLIOGRAPHY

Ali Baba. Emanual Luzzati, 1971. Dist. by Connecticut Films. 16mm. 11 min. Color.

This colorful animated version of *Ali Baba and the Forty Thieves* depicts Ali Baba as a happy-go-lucky lad who cheerfully outwits Mustafa and the thieves.

Amigo by Byrd Baylor Schweitzer, illus. by Garth Williams. Macmillan, 1963.

Longing for a pet dog, a small Mexican boy makes friends with a prairie dog, Amigo, who in turn "tames" the boy. The verse story is illustrated in soft desert pastels.

Anansi the Spider by Gerald McDermott. Holt, 1972.

Adapted from a traditional Ashanti folk tale, this book is based upon the author's film by the same title. Utilizing geometric forms and bold color, it explains why the moon was placed in the sky.

Anansi the Spider. Gerald McDermott Films, 1969. Dist. by Landmark Educational Media. 16mm. 10 min. Color.

Anansi the Spider. Weston Woods, 1973. FS. 43 fr. Color. Cassette. 9.5 min.

Arrow to the Sun by Gerald McDermott. Viking, 1974.

This adaptation of a Pueblo Indian myth tells how Boy searches for his immortal father, the Lord of the Sun. Illustrated with bold color and form, the book won the Caldecott Medal in 1974.

Arrow to the Sun. Gerald McDermott and Texture Films, 1973. 16mm. 12 min. Color.

Arrow to the Sun. Weston Woods, 1975. FS. 36 fr. Color. Cassette. 8.5 min.

Beauty and the Beast by Marianna Mayer, illus. by Mercer Mayer. Four Winds, 1978.

Retold by Marianna Mayer and elegantly illustrated by Mercer Mayer, this book is a fine interpretation of the traditional folk tale about the beautiful daughter who saved her father by agreeing to live in the palace of the beast.

Big Bad Bruce by Bill Peet. Houghton Mifflin, 1977.

Bruce, a bear bully, terrorizes smaller creatures until one day he angers Roxy the witch who diminishes him and keeps him for a pet.

Billy Boy, verses selected by Richard Chase, illus. by Glen Rounds. Golden Gate, 1966.

Glen Round's amusing drawings illustrate this folk song about the wooing of Miss Mary Jane by the mountain lad. Seventeen verses and the piano accompaniment are included.

Billy Boy. Weston Woods, 1970. FS. 39 fr. Color. Cassette. 6 min.

Burt Dow, Deep Water Man by Robert McCloskey. Viking, 1963.

A remarkable tall tale of an old Maine fisherman who escapes a storm at sea by retreating to the belly of a whale. After the storm he escapes from a school of whales by taping a colored bandage on each whale's tale.

Burt Dow, Deep Water Man. Weston Woods, 1983. 16mm. 10 min. Color.

Burt Dow, Deep Water Man. Weston Woods, 1983. FS. 55 fr. Color. Cassette. 17 min.

Casey at the Bat by Ernest Lawrence Thayer, illus. by Paul Frame. Prentice-Hall, 1964.

The famous baseball poem recounting Casey's batting fiasco is humorously illustrated in this picture book.

Casey at the Bat. Weston Woods, n.d. FS. 31 fr. Color. Cassette. 5 min.

Chanticleer and the Fox by Geoffrey Chaucer, adapted and illus. by Barbara Cooney. Crowell, 1958.

Chaucer's "The Nun's Priest's Tale" about the matching of wits by the fox and the rooster is depicted in authentic medieval-flavored detail.

Chanticleer and the Fox. Weston Woods, n.d. FS. 48 fr. Color. Cassette. 10 min.

Clementine by Robert Quackenbush. Lippincott, 1974.

Interpreting this California Gold Rush song as an old-fashioned melodrama, Quackenbush has created a new and appealing twist to the old favorite.

Clementine. Weston Woods, 1975. FS. 40 fr. Color. Cassette. 9.5 min.

Could Anything Be Worse? by Marilyn Hirsh. Holiday, 1974.

In this Yiddish folk tale the rabbi offers advice to a beleaguered man whose household is filled with chaotic noise and fighting. See also *It Could Always Be Worse* by Margot Zemach.

Could Anything Be Worse? Weston Woods, 1975. FS. 33 fr. Color. Cassette. 9 min.

Crictor by Tomi Ungerer. Harper, 1958.

Crictor, a boa constrictor, becomes the pet of sedate Madame Bodot and shows that even a snake can live a useful and valorous life.

Crictor. Weston Woods, 1981. FS. 31 fr. Color. Cassette. 6 min.

Crow Boy by Taro Yashima. Viking, 1955.

Chibi, a young Japanese mountain boy, is taunted and rejected by his classmates until at last they discover his ability to imitate crows.

Crow Boy. Morton Schindel, 1971. Dist. by Weston Woods. 16 mm. 13 min. Color.

Crow Boy. Weston Woods, n.d. FS. 54 fr. Color. Cassette. 7 min.

Don't Count Your Chicks by Ingri and Edgar Parin d'Aulaire. Doubleday, 1943.

Disasters abound when a young woman counts her chickens before they are hatched, dreaming grandiose dreams of what might be.

Don't Count Your Chicks. Weston Woods, n.d. FS. 39 fr. Color. Cassette. 6 min.

The Dragon Takes a Wife by Walter Dean Myers, illus. by Ann Grifalconi. Bobbs-Merrill, 1972.

Lonely Harry the dragon seeks magic from the beautiful swinging fairy Mabel Mae to help him defeat a knight in shining armor and win a wife.

Duffy and the Devil by Harve Zemach, illus. by Margot Zemach. Farrar, Straus, 1973.

Duffy, the maid who can neither spin, weave, nor knit, bargains with the devil for aid. This Cornish variation of the Rumpelstiltskin legend won a Caldecott Medal in 1974.

Duffy and the Devil. Miller-Brody, 1975. FS. 78 fr. Color. Cassette. 17 min.

Erie Canal illus. by Peter Spier. Doubleday, 1970.

Peter Spier has illustrated this folk song about the building of the Erie Canal with historical accuracy and minute detail.

Erie Canal. Morton Schindel, 1976. Dist. by Weston Woods. 16 mm. 7 min. Color.

Erie Canal. Weston Woods, 1974. FS. 27 fr. Color. Cassette. 5 min.

Everyone Knows What a Dragon Looks Like by Jay Williams, illus. by Mercer Mayer. Four Winds, 1976.

When the Wild Horsemen of the North bring war to China, the people of Wu pray to the Great Cloud Dragon for help but fail to recognize him when he arrives.

Fables by Arnold Lobel. Harper, 1980.

This collection of droll one-page stories is illustrated with equally droll one-page paintings. *Fables* was awarded the 1981 Caldecott Medal.

Fables. Random House/Miller Brody, 1981. FS. 135 fr. Color. Cassette. 17 min.

The Five Hundred Hats of Bartholomew Cubbins by Theodore S. Geisel. Vanguard, 1938.

Bartholomew Cubbins' troubles multiply as do his hats which he strives to remove before the king. This folk tale style story offers great possibilities for creative dramatics.

The Fool of the World and the Flying Ship by Arthur Ransome, illus. by Uri Shulevitz. Farrar, Straus, 1968.

In this Russian tale, the third and youngest son wins the Czar's daughter in marriage by producing a flying ship. The book received the 1969 Caldecott Medal.

***The Fool of the World and the Flying Ship*.** Weston Woods, 1979. FS. 56 fr. Color. Cassette. 14 min.

The Foolish Frog by Pete Seeger and Charles Seeger, illus. by Miloslav Jagr. Macmillan, 1973.

Based on an old folk song with illustrations adapted from the film bearing the same name, the book tells of a farmer who makes up a song about a frog and the wonderfully absurd events that result.

The Foolish Frog. Firebird Films, 1971. Dist. by Weston Woods. 16mm. 8 min. Color.

The Foolish Frog. Weston Woods, 1974. FS. 40 fr. Color. Cassette. 9 min.

Fortunately by Remy Charlip. Parents, 1964.

Ned embarks upon a series of adventures which "fortunately" and "unfortunately" aid and hinder his attempts to travel from New York to a Florida birthday party. The outrageously unexpected events will appeal to children of all ages.

Frederick by Leo Lionni. Pantheon, 1966.

Frederick the mouse poet sits by idly while his companions gather food for winter. When the food supply is exhausted, however, he raises everyone's lagging spirit by reciting his poetry.

Frederick. Leo Lionni and Giulio Gianini. 1970. Dist. by Connecticut Films. 16mm. 6 min. Color.

Frederick. Random House, 1974. FS. 46 fr. Color. Cassette. 4 min.

Frog Went A-Courtin' by John Langstaff, illus. by Feodor Rojankovsky. Harcourt, 1955.

The illustrations for this old Scottish ballad of the frog who sought a mouse for his bride won a Caldecott Medal in 1956.

Frog Went A-Courtin'. Morton Schindel, 1961. Dist by Weston Woods. 16mm. 12 min. Color.

Frog Went A-Courtin'. Weston Woods, n.d. FS. 35 fr. Color. Cassette. 13 min.

Frog Went A-Courtin'. Westport Group, 1970. Dist. by Barr Films. FS. 37 fr. Color. Cassette. 3.5 min.

The Funny Little Woman by Arlene Mosel. Dutton, 1972.

This Japanese folk tale tells of a funny little woman who is undaunted by her capture by the fearsome oni, a monster who forces her to cook for him and his friends. The 1973 Caldecott Medal winner.

The Funny Little Woman. Weston Woods, 1973. FS. 38 fr. Color. Cassette. 7 min.

Gabrielle and Selena by Peter Desbarats, illus. by Nancy Grossman. Harcourt, 1968.

Two small girls exchange identities until their clever parents, going along with the game, convince them that each would rather be herself.

Gabrielle and Selena. Stephen Bosustow Productions, 1972. Dist. by BFA Educational Media. 16 mm. 13 min. Color.

The Gift of the Sacred Dog by Paul Gobel. Bradbury, 1980.

A young native American boy seeks help for his people from the Great Spirit and is rewarded with a herd of horses, "Sacred Dogs." Strikingly executed pictures intice the reader to study each page. The simply told story reflects an authentic folklore quality.

The Girl Who Loved Wild Horses by Paul Gobel. Bradbury, 1978.

Winner of the 1979 Caldecott Medal, this beautiful and distinguished book tells of a native American girl who communicated with horses so well that she turned into one.

The Girl Who Loved Wild Horses. Random House/Miller Brody, 1979. FS. 64 fr. Color. Cassette. 9 min.

The Giving Tree by Shel Silverstein. Harper, 1964.

The relationship between a boy and a tree over the boy's lifetime illustrates the nature of love.

The Giving Tree. Stephen Bosustow Productions, 1974. 16mm.

10 min. Color.

The Giving Tree. Stephen Bosustow Productions, 1974. FS. 40 fr. Color. Cassette. 7 min.

Hailstones and Halibut Bones by Mary O'Neill, illus. by Leonard Weisgard. Doubleday, 1961.

Twelve poems, each describing a single color, explore thoughts, feelings, and sensory perceptions.

Hailstones and Halibut Bones: Part I. NBC-TV, 1964. Dist. by Sterling Educational Films. 16mm. 6 min. Color.

Hailstones and Halibut Bones: Part II. NBC-TV, 1967. Dist. by Sterling Educational Films. 16mm. 7 min. Color.

The House on East 88th Street by Bernard Waber. Houghton, 1962.

A crocodile occupies the bath tub in the Primm family's new home in New York City.

The House on East 88th Street. Teaching Resources Films, 1971. FS. 68 fr. Color. Cassette. 15 min.

Howard by James Stevenson. Greenwillow, 1980.

Howard the duck, wintering in New York City instead of migrating, shares a deserted theater with other homeless animals. The city and its famous landmarks are easily identifiable in the humorous illustrations.

New Friends. Made-to-Order Library Productions, 1981. 16mm. 11 min. Color.

I Know an Old Lady Who Swallowed a Fly by Nadine Wescott. Atlantic Monthly/Little, 1980.

The cumulative song about the old lady who swallowed a fly and increasingly larger animals is illustrated in bold stylized drawings.

I Know an Old Lady Who Swallowed a Fly. National Film Board of Canada, 1966. 16mm. 6 min. Color.

I Know an Old Lady. Weston Woods, n.d. FS. 47 fr. Color. Cassette. 6.5 min.

I Know an Old Lady Who Swallowed a Fly; A Cut-and-Paste Flannel Board Story by Nancy Albright. Moonlight Press, 1985.

In a Spring Garden edited by Richard Lewis, illus. by Ezra Jack Keats. Dial, 1965.

Keats has illustrated 23 Japanese nature haiku with striking pictures in collage, watercolor, and line drawing.

In A Spring Garden. Weston Woods, n.d. FS. 28 fr. Cassette. 6 min.

It Could Always Be Worse by Margot Zemach. Farrar, Strauss, 1976.

This Yiddish folk tale of how the Rabbi solves a poor man's noise problem is retold and delightfully illustrated. See also *Could Anything Be Worse* by Marilyn Hirsh.

It Could Always Be Worse. Random House/Miller Brody, 1978. FS. 72 fr. Color. Cassette. 13 min.

Jack Jouett's Ride by Gail E. Haley. Viking, 1973.

Bold woodcuts are used to illustrate Jack Jouett's ride to warn the people of Charlottesville that the British are coming.

Jack Jouett's Ride. Weston Woods, 1975. FS. 34 fr. Color. Cassette. 6.5 min.

John Henry: An American Legend by Ezra Jack Keats. Pantheon, 1965.

Keats' bold illustrations amplify the story of the Black American folk hero, railroad pile driver John Henry.

John Henry. Holt, Rinehart and Winston in cooperation with Lumin Films, 1971. 16mm. 11 min. Color.

John Henry: An American Legend. Guidance Associates, 1967. FS. 45 fr. Color. Cassette. 14 min.

The Judge by Harve Zemach, illus. by Margot Zemach. Farrar, Straus, 1969.

The pompous judge, who jails five innocent persons for describing an approaching monster, gets his comeuppance when the "horrible thing" comes his way.

The Judge. Miller-Brody, 1976. 16mm. 5 min. Color.

The Judge. Miller-Brody, 1975. FS. 47 fr. Color. Cassette. 5 min.

Just Say Hic! Stephen Bosustow Productions, 1969. Dist. by BFA Educational Films. 16mm. 9 min. Color.

This animated film is based on Barbara Walker's version of the Turkish folk tale about the simple-minded boy who takes all directions and advice literally.

The King at the Door by Brock Cole. Doubleday, 1979.

Only Little Baggit believes and responds with kindness to the ragged old man who comes begging at the inn and claims to be the King.

The Legend of Sleepy Hollow. Stephen Bosustow Productions, 1972. 16mm. 14 min. Color.

An animated interpretation of the legend of Icabod Crane and his courtship of the prosperous farmer's daughter, this film captures the spookiness of the Headless Horseman and the mysterious disappearance of Icabod.

Lentil by Robert McCloskey. Viking, 1940.

Lentil, who cannot pucker but can play the harmonica, saves the day for the town by substituting for its band at a celebration for a prominent citizen.

Lentil. Morton Schindel, 1956. Dist. by Weston Woods. 16mm. 8.5 min. Color.

Lentil. Weston Woods, n.d. FS. 42 fr. Color. Cassette. 8.5 min.

Liza Lou and the Yeller Belly Swamp by Mercer Mayer. Four Winds, 1976.

Liza Lou is a heroine's heroine as she outwits one monster after another in the Yeller Belly Swamp.

The Loon's Necklace by William Toye, illus. by Elizabeth Cleaver. Oxford University Press, 1977.

This native American legend tells how the loon, a water bird, acquired its white neckband. Authentic ceremonial masks are used to bring the story to life.

The Loon's Necklace. Encyclopaedia Britannica Educational Corp., 1949. 16mm. 11 min. Color.

The Magic Tree; A Tale From the Congo by Gerald McDermott. Holt, 1973.

Bold, colorful pictures illustrate the story of an unloved boy who finds and then betrays the magic tree which gives him happiness.

The Magic Tree. Gerald McDermott and Texture Films, 1973. 16mm. 10 min. Color.

The Magic Tree. Random House/Miller Brody, 1978. FS. 109 fr. Color. Cassette. 15 min.

Many Moons by James Thurber, illus. by Louis Slobodkin. Harcourt, 1943.

After the king's wise men fail, the court jester succeeds in acquiring the moon to make the little Princess Lenore well again.

Many Moons. Rachel Izel, 1975. Dist. by McGraw-Hill. 16mm. 13 min. Color.

Many Moons. William L. Snyder, 1964. Dist. by Rembrandt Films. 16mm. 10 min. Color.

Once a Mouse by Marcia Brown. Scribner, 1961.

Brown's splendid woodcuts for this Indian fable won a Caldecott Medal in 1962. They depict the hermit who saves a mouse by changing it into larger and larger animals until at last as a royal tiger it must be humbled.

Once a Mouse. Random/Miller Brody, 1977. FS. 42 fr. Color. Cassette. 6 min.

Once Upon MacDonald's Farm by Stephen Gammell. Four Winds Press, 1981.

The absurd, surprise twist to the story of Farmer MacDonald and his animals delights children of all ages.

The Ox-Cart Man by Donald Hall, illus. by Barbara Cooney. Viking, 1979.

Day-to-day life of a nineteenth-century New England farm family is detailed in this extraordinary book. Cooney received the 1980 Caldecott Medal for the illustrations.

The Ox-Cart Man. Viking, 1980. FS. 34 fr. Color. Cassette. 6 min. Dist. by Live Oak Media.

Patrick by Quentin Blake. Walck, 1968.

Patrick buys an old fiddle and magically transforms everything near him with its music.

Patrick. Kratky Film, 1973. Dist. by Weston Woods. 16mm. 7 min. Color.

Poetry for Fun: Trulier Coolier. Centron Films, 1978. 16mm. 11 min. Color.

Appealing verses by Shel Silverstein and other contemporary children's poets are illustrated in a variety of styles ranging from cartoon to live action. The film is ideal for introducing poetry to the uninitiated.

The Princess and the Pumpkin by Maggie Duff, illus. by Catherine Stock. Macmillan, 1980.

Surprises and humor abound in this Majorcan tale of a toothless granny who makes a dying princess well.

Saint George and the Dragon by Margaret Hodges, illus. by Trina Schart Hyman. Little, Brown, 1984.

The 1985 Caldecott Medal book recounts the classic story of the knight St. George who battles the fearsome dragon.

Saint George and the Dragon. Random House, 1985. FS. 90 fr. Color. Cassette. 14 min.

Sam, Bangs, and Moonshine by Evaline Ness. Holt, 1967.

Lonely, motherless Sam creates a fantasy world that becomes almost too real. Only after she causes near disaster for her friend and her cat does she learn the difference "between real and moonshine."

Sam, Bangs, and Moonshine. BFA Educational Media, 1976. 16mm. 15 min. Color.

The Selfish Giant by Oscar Wilde, illus. by Gertraud and Walter Reiner. Harvey House, 1967.

Spring comes to the Giant's garden only when he learns to share it with the children.

The Selfish Giant. Reiner Film, 1971. Dist. by Weston Woods. 16mm. 14 min. B/W.

The Selfish Giant. Murray Shostak and Peter Sander, 1972. Dist. by Pyramid Films. 16mm. 27 min. Color.

The Selfish Giant. Weston Woods, 1972. FS. 39 fr. B/W. Cassette. 12 min.

She'll Be Comin' Round the Mountain by Robert Quackenbush. Lippincott, 1973.

A well-known folk song is transformed into an old-fashioned melodrama complete with villainous train robbers and a beautiful heroine, the prim wardrobe mistress for a Wild West show.

She'll Be Comin' Round the Mountain. Weston Woods, 1975. FS. 40 fr. Color. Cassette. 7 min.

Song of the Swallows by Leo Politi. Scribner, 1949.

The 1950 Caldecott Medal winner, this book beautifully illustrates the annual return of the swallows to Capistrano.

Stone Soup by Marcia Brown. Scribner, 1947.

Three French soldiers teach a group of selfish villagers how to make soup from a stone.

Stone Soup. Morton Schindel, 1955. Dist. by Weston Woods. 16mm. 11 min. Color.

Stone Soup. Weston Woods, n.d. FS. 47 fr. Color. Cassette. 10.5 min.

Stopping By the Woods On a Snowy Evening by Robert Frost, illus. by Susan Jeffers. Dutton, 1978.

This classic verse is uniquely interpreted by lovely illustrations which lure the reader back to pore over each page one more time.

A Story, A Story by Gail Haley. Atheneum, 1970.

A stunning version of the Anansi tale which tells how the Sky God came to release all the stories out into the world, this book received the Caldecott Medal in 1971.

A Story, A Story. Weston Woods, 1973. 16mm. 10 min. Color.

A Story, A Story. Weston Woods, 1972. FS. 40 fr. Color. Cassette. 10 min.

Strega Nona by Tomi de Paola. Prentice-Hall, 1975.

This charming Italian folk tale describes the consequences faced by Big Anthony when he dares to use Strega Nona's magic pasta pot.

Strega Nona. Weston Woods, 1978. 16mm. 9 min. Color.

Strega Nona. Weston Woods, 1978. FS. 55 fr. Color. Cassette. 12 min.

Sylvester and the Magic Pebble by William Steig. Windmill, 1969.

Sylvester Duncan, a young donkey who lives with his parents and collects pebbles of unusual shape and color, finds a magic pebble that grants all wishes. One of his wishes leads to near disaster.

The Three Wishes by Paul Galdone. McGraw-Hill, 1961.

In this folk tale the woodsman receives three wishes, then angers his wife as he unwittingly uses one by idly wishing for a sausage.

Tico and the Golden Wings by Leo Lionni. Pantheon, 1964.

Wingless Tico, granted golden wings by the wishing bird, finds himself still an outcast, dubbed "different" by the other birds. By giving his golden feathers to the needy, Tico acquires black feathers and happiness.

Time of Wonder by Robert McCloskey. Viking, 1962.

Beautiful paintings and poetic text describe summer on a Maine island. The many moods of the sea, the shore, and the weather (including a hurricane) are depicted.

Time of Wonder. Morton Schindel, 1951. Dist. by Weston Woods. 16mm. 13 min. Color.

Time of Wonder. Weston Woods, n.d. FS. 59 fr. Color. Cassette. 13 min.

Troll Music by Anita Lobel. Harper, 1966.
A troupe of musicians, considered the best in the land, are too tired to play for a troll. The troll enchants their instruments which will then only make animal sounds until he is persuaded to remove his spell.

Waltzing Matilda by A.B. Patterson, illus. by Desmond Digby. Holt, 1970.

This ballad, written in 1864, describes the life of a swagman (tramp) in the Australian outback. The intriguing pictures invite the viewer back again and yet again for another look.

Where the Sidewalk Ends by Shel Silverstein. Harper, 1974.

Ranging from slap stick to thought-provoking yet always humorous, the verses of Shel Silverstein are perennial favorites of older children.

Why Mosquitoes Buzz in People's Ears by Verna Aardema, illus. by Leo and Diane Dillon. Dial, 1975.

A chain reaction of events occurs in this West African folk tale when the iguana stuffs sticks in his ears to avoid hearing the mosquito's lies. Interpreted with striking artwork utilizing unique, vivid color, the book won the Caldecott Medal in 1976.

Why Mosquitoes Buzz in People's Ears. Weston Woods, 1984. 16mm. 10 min. Color.

Why Mosquitoes Buzz In People's Ears. Weston Woods, 1976. FS. 43 fr. Color. Cassette. 11 min.

Why The Sun and The Moon Live in The Sky by Elphinstone Dayrell, illus. by Blair Lent. Houghton, 1968.

Blair Lent has depicted this African myth with puppets wearing ceremonial masks to represent the sun, moon, water, and sea creatures.

Why The Sun and The Moon Live In The Sky. ACI Films, 1970. 16mm. 11 min. Color.

Why The Sun and The Moon Live In The Sky. ACI Media, 1973. FS. 67 fr. Color. Cassette. 11 min.

The Woman of the Wood by Algernon D. Black, illus. by Evaline Ness. Holt, 1973.

This adaptation of a Russian folk tale tells of the dilemma existing when a woodcarver, a tailor, and a teacher share in the creation of a beautiful woman and each claim her. The woman chooses, instead, a sage who has declared that no one can own another person.

Zlateh the Goat. Morton Schindel, 1973. Dist. by Weston Woods. 16mm. 20 min. Color.

Based on Isaac Bashevis Singer's short story, the live action film tells of a poor European-Jewish boy's love for his pet goat and how the two help each other survive while lost in a severe blizzard.

INDEX

STORYTELLING AIDS FROM
MOONLIGHT PRESS

Christmas Story Programs by Carolyn S. Peterson and Ann D. Fenton. Illustrated by Christina Sterchele. 1981. 1st ed. rev. $7.00
 ISBN 0-913545-01-5
 A collection of Christmas songs, poems, plays, and finger plays with full-size traceable flannel board and puppet patterns. A bibliography lists picture books, poetry, song books, plays, and professional how-to-books.

Do Tell! Holiday Draw 'n' Tell Stories by Nancy Albright. Revised and enlarged edition. 1987. $4.50 ISBN 0-913545-13-9
 One dozen clever chalk talk stories, each with detailed instructions for sketching simple outline drawings as tale progresses.

Busy Bodies: Finger Plays and Action Rhymes by Marlene Gawron. Rev. ed. 1985. $5.50 ISBN 0-913545-12-0
 Fresh new finger plays arranged under the topics of **Myself, Family, Baby, Food, Play, Nature, Animals,** and **Holidays.** Some in signed English and some with flannel board patterns.

CUT -AND- PASTE SERIES

 Designed for the busy teacher, librarian, child care giver, etc. who needs visua story aids. Printed on colored card stock, ready to cut out and use on the flannel board or as puppets.

I Know an Old Lady Who Swallowed a Fly. Illustrated by Nancy Albright. 1985. $3.50 ISBN 0-913545-10-4

A Hole in the Bottom of the Sea. Illustrated by Christina Sterchele. 1984. $3.50 ISBN 0-913545-09-0

Old MacDonald. Illustrated by Brenny Hall. 1981. $3.50 ISBN 0-913545-04-X

Ten Little Bunnies by Marlene Gawron. Illustrated by Christrina Sterchele. 1981. $3.50 ISBN 0-913545-06-6

The Three Bears. Retold and illustrated by Sally M. Hardy. 1982. $3.50
 ISBN 0-9135-45-08-2